HOT IN PURSUIT

There seemed to be no battle at all. Only a few Comanches firing at the rangers and some shots coming from in among the buildings ahead. Rebecca sat in her saddle, anxious to come to grips with Tulley. Beside her, she heard Captain Slone issue crisp orders.

"Five of you men stay here. The rest come on, after those Comanches. We'll drive 'em out of the canyon and back to the south."

A nearly continuous roar rose as the rangers charged the rear guard. Big Wolf and all his braves died in a matter of seconds and the Texans rode over them, hot in pursuit of Rolling Thunder. Rebecca looked around and saw movement among the ranch structures.

"Down there," she called out. "That looks like Jake Tulley. The gang is getting away." She drew a heavy .44 and urged Ike into a fast trot.

Lone Wolf and Jason hurried after her.

THE DYNAMIC NEW *WHITE SQUAW*
by E. J. Hunter

#1: SIOUX WILDFIRE (1205, $2.50)

Rebecca's uncles offered her to the Sioux in exchange for their own lives. But she survives—through five long years in the Oglala camp—and learns the Indians' cunning ways. Now she's ready to get her revenge and make her uncles pay! She's sexy, daring, and dangerous . . . and nothing will stop her!

#2: BOOMTOWN BUST (1286, $2.50)

When she hears that Bitter Creek Tulley has rounded up his hardcases and is headed for Grub Stake, the new mining boomtown, Rebecca is fast on their trail. She has a plan that's hotter than a pistol!

#3: VIRGIN TERRITORY (1314, $2.50)

When Rebecca finds Jake Tulley's cutthroats in the Ozark hills, she finds *herself*—entirely in their hands. Using her body for bait and her revolver for protection, she bucks the bad guys and evens the score!

#4: HOT TEXAS TAIL (1359, $2.50)

Following the outlaws' scent like a hungry mountain cat, Rebecca rides straight into Galveston, and into the eye of a rip-roaring hurricane. But a lot more than trash and trees will get blown when Tulley's cutthroats come head on against the vengeance-seeking huntress WHITE SQUAW!

Available wherever paperbacks are sold, or order direct from the Publisher. Send cover price plus 50¢ per copy for mailing and handling to Zebra Books, 475 Park Avenue South, New York, N.Y. 10016. DO NOT SEND CASH.

WHITE SQUAW

#4

HOT TEXAS TAIL

BY E. J. HUNTER

ZEBRA BOOKS
KENSINGTON PUBLISHING CORP.

ZEBRA BOOKS

are published by

Kensington Publishing Corp.
475 Park Avenue South
New York, N.Y. 10016

First printing: April, 1984

Printed in the United States of America

This book is dedicated to a tireless worker in the field of factual writing, past and present, a great gal and loyal *aficianada de los toros*; Charlsie Savala of El Paso, Texas.

EJH

On arriving at a large Indian village, the spoils were divided and distributed among the victors. These women fell into the hands of a chief, who transferred them, a short time after. . . . The mother, whose health had broken down under the hardships and sufferings she had endured, was made a common drudge in the camp, while the daughters were appropriated by two warriors and compelled to serve them, both in the capacity of slaves and wives. These women, and doubtless many others like them, are now dragging out their weary lives in misery and captivity.

Three Years Among the Comanches
— Nelson Lee, Texas Ranger

ONE

Johnas Point consisted of five buildings. From miles off on the rolling plains of the Texas Panhandle, approaching riders could see the most prominent, a two-story, thick-walled adobe structure, which housed a trading post that had been added onto haphazardly since the early days of the Texas Republic. Once the only solid structure north and west of San Angelo in Tom Green County, it enjoyed a singular reputation and history. Johnas Point also boasted a livery stable, a blacksmithy, a wheelwright's shop, a feed and grain store, and a saloon. Stubby Tyler at the livery was usually the first one up, ahead even of the roosters who bugled the morn.

Like always, Stubby yawned and stretched and climbed from his cot in the office of the livery on a bright, cool day in late October. He splashed his grizzled face with cold water from a crockery basin and wiped dry on a ragged towel that hung from a wooden peg in the wall. He vowed, as he did three out of every four days, that he would have to get a shave soon. The gray stubble that bristled his chin rasped loudly as he rubbed a work-hardened palm over it. He lit the kindling in a small, potbellied stove to boil water for his coffee, ambled out into the main aisle of the stable and began to fork hay and dole out oats to the inmates of the establishment. From a distance he heard the rattle of wooden shutters and knew that Ab Simmons would be opening the Stone Tank Saloon.

Ab, like all the scant inhabitants of Johnas Point, enjoyed the solitude and peace the small settlement afforded. His potbelly, grown larger since his retirement as a first sergeant in the U.S. Army, swayed as he swung back the louvered wooden shutters that barred entry to his saloon during the closed hours. Rumor had it that there was a trail drive forming up, and he anticipated the increased revenue when the drovers reached Johnas Point. Last saloon until Kansas. That fortuitous fact had often proven the wisdom of his investment. From across the way he saw a black puff of smoke rise from Lester Green's forge and hoped the smith would get around to repairing that damned handtruck. Hauling beer barrels up from the stone cellar by brute strength was a chore he could do without.

Over in the smithy, Lester Green, short, square, and brawny, wiped his hands on a leather apron and looked at the oft-repaired handtruck. If Ab weren't so danged cheap, he'd buy a new one. The way it was, he could see more weld on the axle rod and shaft supports than clean metal. Oh well, Ab was a friend and there wasn't much cash money for Lester to make in a place like Johnas Point. He should be grateful for what he got. In another half-hour, Lester reckoned, the Bieleson brothers would be opening the trading post. He could pick up a box of powdered borax to mix with resin for his welding flux. Might as well get started before Ab set to grumbling about lugging a barrel of beer up from the cellar. Yep, the Bielesons had it set for life with that store of theirs.

Elsie Bieleson had coffee on and bread baking before she awakened her husband, Rupert, their three children, and her brother-in-law, Kurt. Her two sons and daughter clattered noisily out of their room off the storage section of the trading post while Rupert and Kurt clamored down from the second floor living quarters to wash up and have a smoke before breakfast. Horst Bieleson, tow-headed, blue-eyed, and eleven years old, still buttoned his shirt as he ran, barefoot, to the washbasin. Behind him tumbled Frieda, who had only turned nine, her tousled curls swaying around her graceful neck, and Herman, the eight-year-old. On a shelf outside the back door to the shop, the children had their own crockery set and towels for their morning ablutions. Elsie took a deep sniff of the heady aroma of cooking yeasty dough before she turned to receive her husband's kiss, a morning ritual that preceded his washing chores.

That's when Frieda screamed.

Her piercing wail spluttered into words. "*Mutti, Mutti*, they haff an arrow stuck in Herman's belly!"

One hand went to Elsie's pallid cheek and her eyes grew wide with a familiar fear. "*Liebe Gott*, Indians!"

"Inside, children," Rupert commanded as he stepped behind a counter where he kept a loaded Winchester. "*Macht schnell*, and close the door behind you."

"*Aber* . . . Herman," Horst protested as he came on the run.

"Leave him," Rupert snapped. "There is nothing ve can do for him now."

"He . . . he's crying and trying to talk . . ." the frightened little boy yelled in defense of his younger

9

brother. "I can carry him."

"*Und* let safages into the building?" Kurt Bieleson blurted out.

Frieda had cleared the doorway by that time. Horst ignored his uncle's admonition and rushed back to his brother. He lifted the slender child by both shoulders and dragged him toward the door. An arrow whirred past his ear, a terrible, mournful sound of death, and tears flooded his eyes.

"Chust a little more, Hermie," he pleaded. "Push mit your feet."

"C-c-c-an't," came a weak reply.

A rifle bullet split the air near Horst's head and thudded into the solid oak of the door. The brave youngster made a final effort and reached the threshold. Eager hands aided him in pulling Herman inside. The writhing, pain-wracked lad clutched at the feathered shaft with both hands. He moaned and coughed up a gout of blood, then twitched feebly and died. Outside, the shrill war whoops of the Comanche rang with ominous vitality.

Sahonkeno sat his pony in the shallow ravine outside the white-eyes' village and watched the wild approach of his warriors. A satisfied smile curved his thick lips and lighted his black, close-set eyes. His pock-marked cheeks glowed with the excitement of battle lust. So far it had gone exactly as the *Chemakacho* had said it would. But, why should one such as he betray his own kind? Then, why did it matter? It was certainly not something for Fox to worry over. He commanded brave men who would, under direction of the war chief Rolling Thunder, drive the smelly, destructive whites from their land for all time. He would have liked to keep the small, yellow-haired boy for a slave. Perhaps, if the child showed spirit and fight, he would have adopted the whelp to take the place of his own son.

Fox's thoughts brought a hand to his cheek to feel the scars of smallpox that had ravaged him and taken the life of his oldest son off to the Great Spirit. A curse of the whitemen. Like all things bad that had happened to the Comanche since that long-ago time when they had been forced out of the sacred valley of *Mannasaw*. So many moons had gone by that even the oldest among the people no longer remembered that green, fruitful place in the river valley where they gathered through all the summer moons of the grandfather times and no more than three hands count of whitemen had ever been seen. Now it had changed. And *Sahonkeno* vowed to sweep the bad luck of the whites from the land. A rapid burst of shots from one of the white lodges drew his attention. The fires should be starting soon.

"Jesus Christ! It's the heathen Comanch'!" Will Alden, the saloon swamper and town drunk shouted. His gaze froze on the scene beyond the big plate glass window of the Stone Tank Saloon and he dropped his broom from numbed hands. Will thirsted in that moment for a drink like all the tormented souls of hell combined. His whole body trembled and he dashed for where he knew Charlie the bartender kept a sawed-off shotgun under the counter top.

Window glass dissolved in a musical shower under the impact of two slugs and a thrown stone war club. Sawdust rose from the pile where Will dived to save his skin. He shivered in fright and began to crawl toward the bar. His employer came sweating from the cellar, a heavy barrel of beer in his beefy hands. Ab Simmons felt a solid impact against the oak staves that drove him backward to his knees on the top step. Then beer jetted from the side of the container in a foamy stream.

"Bastards!" he shouted at the unseen, howling warriors. "At ten dollars the barrel, you'll ruin me!" He abandoned the emptying container and rushed to where his heavy Springfield hung on the wall of his office.

Ab opened the breech and inserted a fresh cartridge, closed and cocked the weapon and set one hand to scrabbling for additional ammunition. By that time a painted savage face leered at him from the other side of the four-paned window in the back wall of the saloon.

With a quick, though careful shot, Ab erased the face. A gushing spray, driven by internal pressure and Ab's .45-70-405 slug, painted the saloon's outhouse door with the Comanche's blood and brain matter. From the roof above his head, Ab heard an ominous crackling sound and watched as thin tendrils of smoke spurted down into the room.

"Fire!" he heard Lester Green's voice shout from outside. "The devils are burnin' down the town."

Horses whinnied in hysterical despair as six warriors swarmed over the livery. Stubby Tyler let go one barrel, then the second of his Parker shotgun as two of the bare-chested, bronze-skinned braves burst through the tall double doors at the front. The heavy charges of shot blew both men out through the opening, felling a third behind them. Yellow, purple, and grayish coils of intestines spilled from their ripped bellies and big pools of blood began to form. Remarkably, the third savage regained his feet and continued to advance. Stubby snapped open the break-top scattergun and frantically began to reload. Then he became conscious of a sound behind him.

The livery owner spun on one heel in time to take the sharp blade of a steel trade axe in his forehead. It cleaved smoothly through skin and bone and spilled his brains down over his shoulders. Stubby's body convulsed once, mightily, and he fell dead in the center of his stable. The red-painted Comanche, who stood astride of his corpse, knelt and, with dexterous strokes, scalped the dead hostler. In the guttural grunts of his language he set the others to work.

Stubby's horses shrieked in mindless horror as the air inside the barn filled with smoke and flame. Fear overcame gratitude when the saving hands of offensively smelly braves grabbed at their headstalls and fought them to safety.

A frown creased *Nia-ri-u-na's* high forehead. Bullets and arrows smacked into the thick adobe walls of the trading post, yet none seemed to penetrate to the soft flesh of the whites inside. He looked anxiously upward to see if his men had succeeded in reaching the roof. One, he saw with satisfaction, scaled the wall alongside an upstairs' window. Suddenly a rifle barrel protruded from a firing port in the shutter.

Flame and smoke spewed from the muzzle, only an inch from the climbing brave's face. With a strangled cry, the Comanche fell away from the wall. His face had turned black, his eyebrows disappeared, and his hair still flamed when his corpse hit the ground. Wild Horse howled with frustrated hatred for all whites. He had lost another man and for no reason at all. Then he saw feathered scalp locks appear over the peaked roof and a moment later, flames leaped into the morning sky. Better. Now the white-eyes would run out like ants from a hill.

In the feed and grain store, Harmon Teiss bleakly raised the muzzle of his revolver. He fought down an anguished sob and shot his wife and only child precisely in the center of their foreheads. The woman and girl lay twitching out their lives in a puddle of their own gore as Harmon turned to face the press of braves hammering through his front door. He shot the first one an inch below the navel and the second in the groin before his chest became the repository of three arrows. Harmon Teiss coughed up a splash of blood and fell to the floor. Immediately the Comanches swarmed inside.

"The roof is on fire," Kurt Bieleson shouted down the stairs a moment before he came tumbling down onto the trading post counter with a lance shoved in his back.

Frieda screamed and covered her mouth with one hand. Rupert and his son, Horst, continued to fire from loopholes in the rear door and one window. Elsie Bieleson grimly continued to load rifles and hand them to her husband and son. Soon they could all hear the deadly roar of flames.

"Ve haff to get out," Rupert told his family.

"But the . . . Indians," Elsie protested.

"It's take our chances or be burned alive. Ve vill fire out the back until our rifles are empty, then everyone run to the front door. The Comanches vill think ve are still defending the back."

14

Rupert's plan nearly worked. At least none of the family died immediately.

A dozen warriors, led now by Fox, leaped on the fleeing people and bore them to the ground. Hoots of triumph rose from the warriors' throats. Jerked roughly to their feet, the sobbing, struggling Bieleson family heard sounds of shuffling feet, a flat report from an old single-barrel pistol and a scream of agony from the Stone Tank Saloon.

A moment later, three braves dragged Ab Simmons outside. All resistance in Johnas Point had ended.

Gleefully some of the younger warriors and camp boys ripped the clothes from Horst's back. They jerked down his trousers and, before the horrified eyes of his sister and parents, began to sodomize him. The boy shrieked and writhed in the strong hands of his captives, as one after another of the sweaty savages exposed their rigid organs and drove them deep into the cleft of the small, tow-headed boy's buttocks. Suddenly Fox stepped forward.

"Enough. Do not harm him. I, *Sahonkeno*, claim him as my slave."

Looking disappointed at having their fun spoiled, the braves desisted. Horst lay howling in misery on the ground. Fox turned his cruel, close-set eyes on the captives. The corners of his mouth twitched with humor.

"There are the females to pleasure yourselves with," he informed his warriors.

Howls of satisfaction rose. Quickly Ab Simmons and Rupert Bieleson were bound with sticks thrust across their backs, their elbows secured to them by buffalo hide thongs. Their hands, likewise, were bound behind their backs. Then it was Horst's turn. Naked and flaming with shame and agony, the crying boy stood bound beside his father and the saloon keeper as the trio was forced to watch the next event of Comanche entertainment.

Strong hands jerked Frieda off her feet and her clothes quickly became rags on the ground. Four bucks held her down, arms and legs spread wide, while a fifth stepped between her opened thighs and knelt. He jerked up the mid-thigh length hunting shirt favored by the Comanches and revealed his swollen maleness.

Frieda had seen Horst and Herman in the nude on many occasions and had opportunity to observe their appendages dormant and in stages of excitement. Living around farm animals and two brothers, she was fully familiar with the application of these protruding shafts, both for solitary amusement and procreation. Never before, though, had she ever thought to apply their use to her own person. The slender young brave lowered himself and made her aware of it in an insistent, forceful manner.

He thrust the dark red tip of his sleek, fat manhood between the folds of her tightly closed cleft. Frieda felt a heat and pressure never before experienced. Had the circumstances been different, she might have considered it pleasant. Then a searing pain burst inside her as he drove himself deeper. She screamed out her agony as her body seemed to be savagely ripped apart. Unperturbed, the Comanche brave bore in. Lubricated by her blood, he began to drive his hips in a plunging, circular motion until he had inserted all of his throbbing shaft into her unready and unwilling orifice.

Only three powerful strokes in this tightly puckered channel brought the swaying warrior to completion. He howled out his discharge and withdrew. Instantly, another took his place. By now, moistened by savage juices as well as her blood, Frieda had loosened up enough to permit easier entry. She continued to shriek and plead with her tormentors, her slim body writhing

16

on the ground, only adding to their pleasure and lustful anticipating of coming turns. A cold numbness seemed to spread from below her belly button and she lost track of how many surging shafts violated her aching passage.

The only sensations that reached Frieda's tortured brain dealt with stretching, tearing, and sliding. It seemed to go on forever.

When the last, a boy not much older than Horst, shoved and grunted his way to an explosive, satisfying climax in her now thoroughly slippery tunnel, Frieda had mercifully slipped off into unconsciousness. He reluctantly withdrew from her and stood, iron-stiff rod still rigidly erect. His face alight with joy, he howled his delight in his first female conquest in a squeaky voice.

Then the warriors turned their attention to Elsie Bieleson. The raping went on for a long time. Finally they left her dead, a stone axe used to split her skull. Terse orders from Fox set the raiding party into action.

The captives, Rupert and Horst Bieleson, Ab Simmons, and little Frieda Bieleson had deerskin bags pulled over their heads for blindfolds, then set upon the bare backs of mules from the livery stable. Their hands remained bound and buffalo hide thongs tied their ankles together under the bellies of the animals. When everything reached Fox's satisfaction, he raised his feather-decorated lance above his head and called out loudly to the warriors.

"We must hurry to meet with *Kansaleumko* and the *Chemakacho*."

TWO

Broad buttocks resting on the weathered boards of a wagon seat, Bitter Creek Jake Tulley stared about the wide, undulating, treeless land of the Texas Panhandle. If he hadn't been there, seen it with his own eyes, he would never believe that his fortunes could have sunk so low. The bed of the buckboard was filled with cases of cheap, rot-gut whiskey, trade blankets, boxes of ammunition, and a stack containing two dozen oil-paper-wrapped rifles. Shit, he fumed, reduced to trading with the Injuns again. He slammed his black bowler hat against the dashboard, exposing thinning tufts of his reddish-brown hair.

"Dammit, Roger," he expressed his discontent aloud. "Every time I think of that rotten bitch it makes my blood boil. If it weren't for Rebecca Caldwell, we wouldn't be out here waitin' for a bunch of savages to ride up an' maybe kill us instead of make an open trade."

Roger Styles, dapper, impeccably dressed in a

conservatively cut gray suit, lace-trimmed white shirt, and red satin vest, turned a disdainful expression on his companion. His lips quirked in a superior, almost smirking, smile. Of late, he had come to the conclusion that Jake had nearly outlived his usefulness. It seemed that misfortune stalked the thick-set outlaw. Yes. Misfortune in the shape of Rebecca Caldwell. Their association had been a long and sometimes profitable one. Yet, the implacable pursuit of the half-Sioux girl threatened to end it. Roger fully intended not to be a part of their crime partnership's demise.

"You didn't have to come along, Jake. You're the one who insisted that you and Opie be here when I met with Fox."

"We's partners, ain't we?" Jake grumbled. "What I can't figger is how you learned to palaver with these Comanche. So, I thought it a good idea to come along and see what our investment is buyin' us," he finished lamely.

"You don't trust me?" Roger inquired in a wounded tone.

"I don't trust those *goddamned redskins*!" Jake flared back. Then he returned to his original topic. "Maybe we shoulda never traded that Rebecca an' her Maw off to the Sioux."

"Ummh?"

"Or maybe we oughta stood firmer in Grub Stake. You know? There was more of us than her and her handful of whiners."

"The scandal it would have aroused would have ruined my plans for public office all the same," Roger replied.

"But she an' that goddamned white Injun she rides with woulda been six feet under," Jake protested. "Only no, we cut and run and gave them a chance to

20

track down that wagon train of li'l girls we was gonna sell to them fat-gutted A-rabs. I suppose you wouldn'ta minded taking a swing at some o' that young snatch, eh?" Jake eyed his partner shrewdly.

"Only if they fought me a little, dear boy."

"Huh?"

"'Any sissy can have a seduction,'" Roger quoted primly. "'But a he-man wants his rape.' One thing positive I can say about your dear Rebecca Caldwell, she was good. Exceptionally good. Fought like a wildcat when I raped her."

"Good huh? Last I recall, she kicked you in the balls and started that buffalo stampede."

Roger winced at the reminder and sent his gaze off over the rolling prairie toward a dark swath that indicated a deep ravine. A thin haze of brown rose from its depths. "Our, ah, clients will be here shortly."

When Fox rode up at the head of his raiding party and clutch of prisoners, he held his war lance in his left hand, the right extended, palm up in the universal plains sign talk indicating peace.

"Ho, *Chemakacho*," he greeted Roger.

"Heya, *Sahonkeno*. We have brought much whiskey, blankets, ammunition."

"You bring rifles?"

"Yes, of course." Roger climbed from the wagon and approached the warrior. "Did you bring many yellowmetal pieces . . ." He reached up behind Fox's left ear and, by sleight of hand, produced a twenty dollar gold piece. "Like this?"

Several braves muttered in astonishment at this show of powerful magic. Fox's eyes widened slightly, the only sign of his own surprise. Then his pinched face seemed to lengthen and a sorrowful expression tugged at his pock-marked cheeks.

"Whiteman lodges burned before we could look for many of the yellow-metal discs. Next time . . ."

Roger's usual suave aplomb deserted him for a moment. "Next time? Damnit, Fox, what the hell do you think we're supplying you for? We want the gold!" Frustrated, he resorted to English, his limited Comanche vocabulary not sufficient to express his feelings. "Can't you get that through your empty, savage head? Gold, you motherless lump of filth."

Although the words meant nothing to him, Fox slitted his close-set eyes and his jaw jutted in firm anger. At sight of this, Roger mustered his raving temper and drew a deep breath.

"Ah . . . yes. Next time. And that will come soon. There are few people at Cullum Tank, the white village only two sleeps from here. But there is a lot of the yellow-metal discs. Some of my men will ride with you to see that you bring it all. Whatever you have with you will be good enough . . . for now. Jake, you and Opie unload the supplies for our good friend Fox here. That's a good man. Now . . ." Roger turned back to Fox, his eyes alight with avarice. "What did you manage to bring?"

As he worked, smarting under Roger's superior attitude, Jake noticed the prisoners. "What'er them dummies done up in them bags for?" he inquired.

"Prisoners," Roger told him, then questioned Fox.

"White-eyes from village we raid, *Chemakacho*," the war party leader told him. "We take them to main camp of *Kansaleumko* for big war dance."

"What's that mean?" Jake pressed after Roger interpreted.

"Probably that they will be tortured to death."

"Uh . . . oh. An' what's that Chema-whatits he calls you?"

"It means Good White Man. Rather fitting, don't

you think?"

"Good! It's . . . so . . . very . . . GOOD!" Rebecca
Caldwell panted out over the rhythmic creaking of the
bed springs. She thrilled to the powerful surges of the
thick, pulsing shaft that threatened to divide her in two
from her burning, vibrating cleft to her chin as it slid
demandingly, unceasingly through the moist passage.
It took all her concentration and deft skill to expand
enough to encompass that marvelous organ of delight.
Two months in New Orleans and, since the earliest
days of Philipe DuBois' convalescence, not a day without that ponderous presence deep inside her.

"AAAH! . . . Philipe! . . . Don't! . . . Stop! . . .
NOW!" she shrieked as yet another wave of completion
crashed over her and washed away all sensation outside
of blinding ecstasy. Oh, God, how wonderful it was to
be a woman, she thought as her head thrashed from
side to side on the silk pillow. Nothing in the world
could compare with the wondrous exhilaration that
electrified her body at such times. She had a passionate
nature, her mother had told her from earliest child-
hood. As the beautiful, black-haired girl plummeted
off the latest pinnacle, she reflected on how, over her
growing years, she had employed a wide variety of
experiments to plumb the depths of her liquid pool of
fire.

Then, after the flood gates had been burst asunder by
a handsome, exciting Oglala boy named Four Horns,
she had found her volcano of passion to be unquench-
able. She loved loving and lived for each night when
her husband, that same delightful Four Horns, came to
her sleeping robes and they joined in the heavenly
combat. Never, she believed, would any man fully

envelop her needs. Until she met Philipe, that surety remained intact.

For the first time in her nearly nineteen years of life, Rebecca found her desires fulfilled with each mingling of their bodies and souls. Yet the contentment lasted only a short while. Each day saw new urgency burning hotly in her breast, her skin tingling and sensitive to the touch at the mere thought of that powerful lance that speared her to the heart. Her velvet purse ran wet and trembled for the magic touch. Her thoughts kaleidoscoped away in shards of blazing colored light as she, along with her skillful and attentive lover, crescendoed together and subsided, gasping and dizzy on Philipe's big bed.

Long moments passed before Rebecca spoke as her small, firm hand encircled the thick base of Philipe's penis which was still rigid. "No wonder they chose the name, 'organ.' This one certainly makes music inside me."

"You are poetic today, *mon petit cher*."

"It's you, Philipe. You make me want to sing and set me all to trembling inside waiting for your love."

Philipe stirred his slender body then, making preparations for their next engagement. Gently he lifted Rebecca, placed a thick bolster under her hips, and with her willing help, spread her legs wide. He knelt between the silken, pale-bronze columns of her thighs and lowered his bobbing manhood until it made the lightest of contacts at the top of her moist cleft. With one hand, he began to direct his turgid phallus downward with only the slightest of penetration. He continued the delightful teasing, up-down, up-down, while Rebecca tried valiantly to impale herself on that fiery shaft.

"Ummmm. That's so sweet of you, Philipe."

"Like it?"

"I like everything you do. Only . . . only, now you must hurry, my dearest. I don't think I can s-stand t-this m-m-much longer!"

Strength, not length, was Philipe's main suit, though he made up for depth with a wedgelike girth and force that never failed to pop wide Rebecca's startlingly deep blue eyes. He used the improved angle of approach that the bolster provided to heighten this effect as they joined again in a renewal of the infinite *combat d'amour*.

The happy couple waged five amorous battles throughout the long afternoon. Spent at last, Rebecca rose in early evening, unhurried as she crossed to a dressing table to put up her hair. No one dined in New Orleans before nine, so she would be able to return to her hotel, dress, and be ready when Philipe called to take her to the *Maison Provincial*. In search of a comb, she opened the middle drawer of the commode and looked down on a newspaper.

Bold headlines burned into her consciousness:

COMANCHES TERRORIZE NORTHWEST TEXAS
TWENTY FEARED DEAD AT JOHNAS POINT

and below an advertisement for women's millinery fashions:

CULLUM TANK MASSACRE

She turned to Philipe who had come into the bedroom from his closet.

"Philipe, what is this?"

"Uh . . . nothing, my dear. An old, uh, newspaper."

"Not so old. Four days ago in Beaumont, Texas. Why . . . why did you hide this from me?"

"I . . . I didn't hide it, *mon amour*. I merely didn't

want you to see . . . ah, to have it upset you."

"Philipe!" Rebecca cried, her cobalt eyes flashing with dangerous sparks. "You know how important such news is to me. You surely realize how badly I need to be informed. This . . . this reeks of Jake Tulley."

"Indian raids? Isn't that stretching a bit?"

"I don't know why. I only . . . feel it is somehow connected." She looked at a third article on the advertising-crowded front page. "Here. It says that survivors of the Cullum Tank raid stated positively that white men were along with the Comanche braves. Now do you see?"

"Not really," Philipe tried to depreciate. "That's not unusual . . . or new. The Comanche are noted for taking a lot of prisoners. In the case of children, they are often raised by the tribe."

"But these were not children, or stripling boys. See? It says right here that 'several grown men, speaking English, were along with the hostiles.' Children raised by Indians do not continue to use English. Believe me, I know."

"Now, now, you're getting excited, dear Rebecca. Your past experiences, living with the Sioux, your encounters with Jake Tulley . . . all of this has been trying. I'm sure there is no connection whatsoever. Trust me in this."

"Trust you! You hid the paper from me. You tried to shield me from finding out. If you, yes, *you* didn't suspect there might be some connection, why did you find that necessary?"

Philipe crossed the thick Persian carpet and reached out to embrace her. "Please, my love, you're getting upset."

"You're damned right I am. How many other times in the past six weeks have you acted to 'protect' me from myself."

"That's unfair," Philipe began, to be interrupted by a furious splutter from Rebecca.

"You are the one being unfair! Am I a child to be kept ignorant of such matters? Look at me. I've killed more than fifteen men, Philipe." She shook her head in exasperation. "I've quit counting how many. You were along when I finished off a couple of Tulley's men on board that ship. Do I appear to you to be incapable of handling my own affairs? I want Jake Tulley. I want his head on a pole. No one . . . not even you . . . are going to stand in the way of that."

Again Philipe attempted to embrace her. Rebecca brushed his arms aside, rose, and stalked to the door. "I love you, *mon couer*," Philipe cried, wounded by her anger.

"And I love you, Philipe. More than any man I've known. And it's not just the, uh, physical . . ." In spite of her fury, her insatiable passion notwithstanding, Rebecca managed to blush. "Only this thing is inside me, demanding, driving. I must get revenge. I *will* get it. I c-can't . . . put words to . . . to what I feel when I think of Roger Styles' filthy hands pawing my body, humiliating and shaming me. I want his death at my own hands. Nothing else will do. I . . . I'm sorry, Philipe. This is my . . . my destiny, my *hmunga* as the Oglala say, a great mystery to be feared."

"If you fear it, abandon it," Philipe pleaded.

Rebecca looked at the handsome, beloved young man as though she had never seen him before. "Philipe, Philipe, that is like saying I could abandon breathing. I'm sorry, dearest Philipe. I'm going to find Lone Wolf. I must look into this. *I must find out*."

THREE

"Just a little further, *amigo*, and then you can take off that blindfold." The speaker held the reins to Roger Styles' horse and led him through the maze of a boulder-strewn canyon. They had been traveling in this manner for half an hour and now, Roger's straining ears detected a jumble of sound in the distance and his nostrils sniffed the odor of cooking meat.

"Around this bend an' we're there," his guide informed Roger.

"Was all of this really necessary?" Roger inquired peevishly.

"Them was my orders," the surly escort growled.

At least, Roger thought, he would finally be in the main camp of the Comancheros. A scruffy lot, he reflected. Renegade whites and Mexicans, a few blacks who had drifted in after emancipation, or joined earlier as escaped slaves. They conducted a sort of trade with the Comanches, hence the name. Often it involved female hostages. According to that braggart Horning, who bossed one contingent of the men he had come to recruit, some Comancheros had grown rich selling horses stolen by the Indians to their former owners. He would soon see if their reputation exceeded their abilities. His mount made a sudden halt and, sightless, Roger nearly pitched from the saddle.

"You can take that kerchief off yer face now," the man who called himself Nolan told him.

Eyes watering at the sudden brightness, Roger blinked, then gaped at the incredible scene that spread through a wide box canyon ahead of him. Blue-white smoke rose in thick clouds above a huge fire pit off to the right. Over the shimmering coals and flickering flames, long skewers revolved, turned by the hands of patient, small brown boys who crouched, all but naked, on their bare feet and slowly rolled the meat. One iron shaft held an exceptionally large side of beef, while three others bore the whole carcasses of two goats each. Everywhere, men, women, and children hurried about unknown tasks and dust rose in the air. From the far end of the camp, against the base of the canyon wall, a wild yell drew Roger's attention.

Horses thundered toward them, the riders flailing their mounts' hind quarters with rawhide quirts. People leaped out of their way and Nolan shouted to Roger over the tumult.

"By God, I hope Bob does it this time. I done bet five dollars on him before I left to fetch you. He's got the best horse, ya know."

"Someone could get killed, racing like this," Roger observed and immediately knew that it might be him.

After the foaming-mouthed beasts rumbled past them, relative quiet returned. "He did it!" Nolan exulted, standing in his stirrups to see the end of the race.

"Congratulations," Roger offered dryly. A high-pitched squeal of delight turned Roger's head to the left.

"Oooh. Do it! Do it harder. Aaaah . . . sooo good!"

A girl, who to Roger appeared to be no more than fourteen or fifteen, lay writhing on a blanket while a buckskin-clad Comanchero drove his stiff rod deep into her, his bare, pale-white buttocks churning in the sunlight. Three other rakishly garbed members of the band stood by, their trousers already open. They idly fondled their elongated organs while they waited their turns.

"Who is that?" Roger inquired of his guide.

"Some girl we bought from the Comanches. She's sure a good fuck. Loves it, too."

"So I observed. Shall we get on to Mister Horning and Mister Gonzales?"

"Yup. Right this way. We'll leave the horses at that pole corral."

Slender trees that grew tall and thin in the shadowed canyon had been cut to build a large corral to hold working stock and animals for sale or trade. The two men looped their reins over the top rail, and Nolan led the way to a large, brush-roofed, open pavilion. A hard-bitten pair sat at a square wooden table under the shade, matching each other shot for shot from a clay bottle of tequila. Roger recognized Alex Horning, who wore the same food-stained buckskin trousers and faded wool shirt as on their first encounter. The white Comanchero had an ugly knife scar on his right cheek that ran in a tight curve from the corner of his eye to a point below his lower lip. He affected a tobacco-stained, full-flowing mustache that drooped around his mouth in a manner suggestive of the back end of a mule, and a black leather vest, from which suspended small wisps of human hair—trophies of his years of lawlessness.

Across from him sat a whippet-lean Mexican. Gonzales, Roger surmised. He wore whipcord trousers of a russet-brown color, lace-front white shirt, soiled

31

by food and liquor, and a matching, long-sleeved, waist-length jacket. The largest, most ornately silver-decorated sombrero Roger had ever seen sat on the slender Mexican's sleek head, rakishly tilted back to expose a high forehead. A pencil-line mustache graced Gonzales' upper lip and a finger-thick shock of equally black hair curved under his chin from its origin on his lower lip. He glared hatred at Roger as the latter approached.

"I am Roger Styles," the would-be empire builder announced unnecessarily. "I have come to offer you gentlemen a place in history."

"Cut out the sheet, *señor*, and get down to business," Gonzales snarled.

"Uh . . . yes . . . certainly. Essentially, what I plan is to carve out an empire for my . . . ah, for us, from the Panhandle of Texas. As you know, the area is sparsely settled by Americans and many of the hostiles have already gone to other places."

"What's to say we don't ventilate your young ass and build this empire ourselves?" Horning wanted to know.

"Ah . . . well, if you gentlemen had've possessed the organizational skills and political connections to insure such a scheme, I assume you would have already done it. I know which government people to bribe . . . in Texas and in Washington City. I have powerful contacts in Colorado. Influence, Mister Horning, *Señor* Gonzales. That is the key to this sort of power."

"While you are using thees influence, what do you think the Texas Rangers weel be doing?" Gonzales sneered.

"Texas is a large place. There is only one battalion of Rangers to police the whole state. We will have a superior force, once your men ride under my banner and the Comanches—who are already raiding where and when I say—continue to lend support." Roger deliberately omitted mention of the Bitter Creek Jake

Tulley gang. Never wise, he believed, to lay all of his cards on the table at the same time. "Surely the governor and the commandant of the rangers will see the wisdom in not wasting lives needlessly in an uneven contest. The Panhandle is not so much. It could hardly be missed."

Gonzales snorted and gulped down another shot of tequila. Horning followed suit and studied Roger like a specimen in a laboratory.

"I don't like this prissy *cabrón*," Gonzales hissed in a loud whisper while he poured more of the fiery white liquor.

Horning grunted and waved away the remark with an impatient gesture. "You make it sound so easy, Styles. Frankly, I think you are full of shit. Pablo and I agreed to talk to you because the idea did sound profitable to us. Lots of loot to be taken, all of that. But you can't be serious in believing that you can simply *take* some three thousand square miles and not have the army and the rangers down on you? Why hold on to it? Squeeze it dry of everything that can be converted to cash and get the hell out."

"But . . . the *land* is money," Roger protested. He sensed that he was losing control. "Besides," he quoted, "'possession is nine parts of the law.' If we hold the land, we can legitimately claim it."

"Well, right now a whole big goddamned chunk of it is bein' claimed by Charlie Goodnight," Horning told him.

"Who's that?"

"Colonel Charles Goodnight. He an' Oliver Loving broke a trail to Colorado a few years back, made a mint sellin' cattle. Now he's fixin' to put a herd in Palo Duro Canyon. He's one tough son of a bitch, with the foulest mouth I've ever heard."

Roger blinked. He rarely used profanity and such an observation from a man like Horning gave him cause to wonder. He disregarded the comment and pressed his argument. "We can file claim on much of the unoccupied land, force sales, run people off. At least we can once we have the manpower. Once we have the papers . . ."

"*Papers?*" Gonzales interrupted. "Who needs any steenking papers? We got guns, we got men, we *take* what we want."

"And run from the rangers every time?" Roger made bold to remind both bandit leaders. "My way you will have a haven. A separate country if you will. No jurisdiction by the rangers. Think of it."

Before either Comanchero made an answer, a shrill, terrified cry rose from a brush hut. "*No! Madre de Dios, ayudame, por favor.* Don't do this," the pleading voice went on in Spanish. "My woman, my children . . . *ay* have mercy."

Four of Gonzales' Mexican Comancheros dragged a rail-thin man, dressed in peon's white cotton trousers and long-sleeved shirt, from the hut and hauled him to a place where two stout posts had been driven into the ground. Long rawhide thongs dangled from the trimmed pines. Deftly the brigands tied his hands high above his head and bound his ankles so that he hung spread-eagled between the uprights. Then they stepped back, laughing.

Three of them drew their revolvers and cocked the hammers. As Roger watched uneasily, they began a grim contest of target practice. With each shot and the meaty impact of the slug, the frail Mexican screamed in agony. Between rounds he sobbed uncontrollably. The pistoleros needed the practice, Roger thought. They came far from striking a vital spot. At last, one gunman put a bullet in the unfortunate man's forehead.

"Pedro, you *estúpido*, now you have spoiled all our fun," one Comanchero complained to the accurate one. The comment caused Roger to shudder.

The men under the brush pavilion turned away from the scene of torture. Gonzales poured more tequila and explained. "A spy. We caught him the night before we rode here to meet with you. He has paid . . . though not so much as my men would have liked, no?"

Roger swallowed hard. "I'll ask you gentlemen again to consider my proposition. If we work together, we can amass vast fortunes. The plan will work. Trust me."

"We trust no one, *señor*," Gonzales told him blandly. "Not even ourselves. All the same, yes, I theenk I weel consider what you say carefully."

"Me, too," Horning agreed. "We'll let you know within a week. Now, Nolan here can escort you out of the canyon. We've got a lot of drinkin' and eatin' to do."

Dismissed so summarily, Roger could do nothing but stumble back to his horse.

A steam whistle shrilled a warning to well-wishers as the last passengers negotiated the gangplank to board the side-wheeler steam packet, *La Belle Marie*. Unhappy at the prospect of a sea voyage, Lone Wolf carried his luggage and Rebecca's to their cabins. Rebecca saw her portmanteau in place, locked her door, and went hopefully to the rail.

She had not seen nor heard from Philipe since their quarrel the previous day. Disappointment filled her. She truly loved him, yet she feared she had become so obsessed with the idea of revenge on Jake Tulley that she remained blinded to nearly everything else.

"All passengers from New Orleans to Galveston aboard, please," a uniformed officer called through a megaphone at the people gathered on the dock. "Sailing in ten minutes. All aboard, please." He repeated the announcement in French.

Rebecca scanned the faces in the small crowd. Nowhere did she see Philipe DuBois. A pain clutched at her heart. The whistle shrieked again and black smoke poured from the tall stack as fuel was fed to the boiler by sweating coalers. Four crewmen swayed the gangplank aboard and the iron-clad vessel shuddered its length as the shaft turned and the big paddle wheels began to revolve. Other deck hands cast off the bow line, then the stern, and *La Belle Marie* swung out into the stream of the muddy Mississippi. Disappointment clouded the excitement of departure for Rebecca. She started to turn away from the rail when a shout stopped her.

"Becky! *Mon cher*, Rebecca!"

Rebecca turned back. A flash of happiness made her dizzy. Philipe, flowers in hand, stood on the pier, watching as the ship drifted away. "Philipe . . . I . . . I'll miss you."

"*Au revoir!* Come back to me, my love. Come back when . . . when you are done."

Rebecca waved and felt moisture gathering in her eyes. Oh, how she wanted to say yes. Though she knew that such a thing would never be. And . . . already she missed Philipe with a terrible longing. A short distance down the deck, an attractive woman in her late twenties sniffed disdainfully.

"Well, I never," she spoke to a young man at her side. "These utterly demonstrative foreigners. A Frenchman, by the sound of it. It's so . . . *continental*, I know, but for the life of me, Jason, I cannot fathom such public goings-on. Most *déclassé*, don't you think?"

"You are over critical, Priss. Different places, different ways, don't you know?" The young man's British accent matched the woman's for quality and refinement.

"Isn't that bunch a show in themselves?" Lone Wolf asked as he came up quietly beside Rebecca.

"You know them?"

"Not so's to be on first name terms. He's some sort of lord or the likes. She's Lady Priscilla Parrish. She's got a husband along, though the way she clings to that young feller, Lord Jason, you wouldn't hardly know it."

Rebecca took time to carefully examine the pair. Lady Priscilla was tall and slender, with perhaps a bit too much neck. She had large breasts, that the current fashions failed to adequately conceal, and wide-set, pale blue eyes that seemed icy and aloof. She must be a good five years older than the man, Rebecca thought. Her taffy-blonde hair had been twisted into a large roll and tucked up under a modish, wide-brimmed hat.

Jason, on the other hand, looked not the least unapproachable. He had a firm, clean jaw line, a ready smile that revealed even white teeth and a luxurious, thick thatch of dark auburn hair. His vivid green eyes twinkled with ready merriment. She judged that he might be a bit soft around the middle, from good living, but his hands were squarish, with blunt fingers and well-tended nails.

"He's really quite handsome, isn't he?" she remarked to her companion.

Lone Wolf, who had been known as Bret Baylor before his abduction by the Crow, declined comment. This fancy English lord had a certain weakness about his mouth which, to his way of seeing things, suggested a spoiled, pampered nature, though he had a sturdy enough build, Lone Wolf allowed. Good shoulders and apparently some muscle inside those tight sleeves. Young, too. He figured Jason for perhaps twenty-two or three years old.

A young boy came trotting up to the English couple.

"Uncle Jason," he piped in a high, pure tone. "This is nothing like the ship we came over in, is it? I do hope we have an exciting trip. Will there be wild Indians in this Texas place?"

"I suppose so, Chris," Lord Jason replied. "You run along now to the bow and watch the trip down the river to the gulf."

"Straight away, Uncle Jason," the lad replied. He turned and hurried toward where Rebecca and Lone Wolf stood.

"Uh, hullo," he greeted them, removing a slouched, cloth cap. "I'm Christopher Anderson. That's my uncle, Jason Plumm, Lord Southington, and the Lady Priscilla Parrish. She's a pain," he confided in a lowered voice.

"Glad to know you, Christopher. I'm Lo . . . uh, Bret Baylor and this is Miss Rebecca Caldwell."

Christopher bowed slightly. "Pleasure to make your acquaintance, Miss Caldwell, Mister Baylor. I hope to see more of you during our voyage. We're going to Texas to hunt bison and other big game."

"How interesting," Rebecca said, secretly amused at the bright youngster's brash enthusiasm. He had brownish-blond hair that partly covered his ears, a slightly narrow, though open and honest face, with blue-gray eyes and a high, smooth forehead. She decided she liked him a great deal. "It sounds like you will have a lot of adventure."

"Oh, I certainly hope so. You'll have to excuse me now. I must go forward and watch these dismal swamps. Quaint country, America, isn't it rather?" The boy replaced his cap and scampered off along the deck.

"He seems like a nice boy," Lone Wolf observed.

"Yes." Her eyes glided sideways to take in Christopher's uncle. "His uncle seems a nice enough sort, too. Doesn't he?"

FOUR

The steam packet, *La Belle Marie*, had a single dining salon. Three long tables took care of the needs of crew, steerage passengers, first class, and the ship's officers. After the assistant purser had gone through the vessel, sounding a gong to announce the evening meal, and people began to assemble, Lady Priscilla Parrish made several observations in a strident voice.

"Don't tell me that *those* people are eating in the same room with our class?" she demanded of the purser, indicating the crewmen.

"Why certainly, Madam. There is no other place."

"I suppose our servants will be here also," she added in a snippy observation.

"Of course. They *are* carried on the manifest as steerage passengers. Theirs will be the center table. Is there anything that Madam, ah, desires?" A mousy man, the purser hoped to avoid any sort of unpleasantries.

"Certainly arrangements can be made to serve these

menials below decks? Their presence offends my finer sensibilities," Priscilla told him imperiously.

"But . . . that is totally impossible. There is no room, not even tables or chairs to set out. Every cargo hold is full."

"Our servants can eat standing up among the boxes and bales, so can your crew," Priscilla decided in a tone that invited no further defiance. "You Americans are pursuing a disastrous course with your passion for egalitarianism. Ultimately you will produce a nation of nothing but . . . trash."

Stung by her haughty, insulting manner, the purser drew himself up to his full five foot three height and fixed her with a baleful glare. "I am sorry, Madam, but what you request can not be done. This is the dining salon and this is where we all shall eat."

"I will speak to the captain about your insolence, my man," Priscilla snapped.

"Do so, Madam . . . at your own peril," came the icy reply. The purser turned on one heel and stalked away.

A moment later the captain entered and Lady Priscilla swept down on him with a light of combat in her eyes. She quickly made known her requirements, simple enough to her, then launched into a scathing denunciation of the purser. When she finished, the captain examined her coolly, like some particularly unpleasant specimen brought up from the depths of the sea.

"My purser was quite right, Lady Priscilla. I make such decisions on board this ship, not the passengers. You are neither an owner nor an officer of the line. If you wish to avoid the unpleasant experience, as you describe it, of rubbing elbows with the hoi polloi, I suggest you take your meals in your cabin. Otherwise, please confine your opinions to yourself. Now, if you will excuse me, I must meet our other first class passengers."

Left open-mouthed in astonishment, Lady Priscilla flounced to the chair where a place card indicated her seat for dinner.

"I've learned a little more about our fellow passengers," Lone Wolf told Rebecca as they entered the salon. The both wore white man's clothing and felt uncomfortable for it. Only first class accommodations had been available when they booked passage at so late a date, so they would be joining the British party at the captain's table.

"Anything interesting?" Rebecca prompted.

"A bit. That stocky feller over there." He indicated a long-faced, balding man in a black suit who sat at the head of the middle table. "He's Riggs. Your Lord Jason's man."

"His man?"

"'A gentleman's gentleman,' is how he describes it. He takes care of Plumm's personal effects, arranges appointments, supervises the household, that sort of thing." Lone Wolf laughed. "I don't rightly know exactly what all that means, but that's what he said he did for 'his Lordship.' He's friendly enough and seems genuinely interested in the country they're headed for."

"Where's that?"

"The Texas Panhandle," Lone Wolf told her with a twinkle in his eyes.

"Why . . . and you've been cultivating this, ah, Riggs?" Rebecca asked, ideas already spinning in her head.

"Thought it might not hurt."

"Good. Go on. What else have you discovered?"

"Young Christopher isn't alone in his dislike of Lady

Parrish. She and her husband don't get along well and no one else likes her much, either. She is twenty-nine, he's thirty-seven. Seems, at least to Riggs, that she has her head set on an affair with Lord Southington. By the way, on this trip to 'quaint' North America, as Lady Priscilla calls it, Lord Southington prefers to be called by his family name. Jason Plumm. He's a good sportsman, according to Riggs, an excellent shot. He's hunted game in the Egyptian desert, India, the African veldt. Now he wants to 'try on' America."

"Why didn't they go to Canada, then? That's English, isn't it?"

"He wants to take a grizzly, a buffalo, antelope, and a mountain lion. Things that are in short supply in Canada according to Riggs. The distinguished old fellow sitting down on Plumm's right is Sir Devon Windemire. He oversees Plumm's finances, investments, he's what they call a noble squire in England. There's some land and a village or two involved, from what I gather, and Sir Devon administers justice and directs the work there for Plumm. Riggs considers that, since Plumm reached his majority two years ago, Sir Devon is still taking too much active interest. He's an avid hunter, though, and accompanies Plumm on all of his expeditions.

"Then, of course, there is Christopher Anderson. He's Plumm's sister's boy. Her husband is involved in the House of Lords in London and Plumm thought the lad should see a bit of the world outside chimney pots and tenements, as Riggs called it. The boy is bright, but has a serious side. He has a sister, much younger, and Plumm was only two years older than the boy when he inherited his title and estates. So, Plumm has a strong feeling for him.

"That sums up the family. Then, there's Monson, that red-faced man. He's the cook. The sissifiedlooking fellow with spectacles is Basil, the wine steward . . . whatever that is. The frightened-looking girl sitting next to Basil is Effie, Lady Priscilla's maid."

"Is there anything you don't know?" Rebecca asked, amazed at what all Lone Wolf had been able to learn.

"Only how soon you are going to forget your Frenchman and fall for Jason Plumm," he shot back teasingly.

"You!" Rebecca elbowed Lone Wolf sharply in the ribs as the purser came forward to escort them to the captain's table.

After the meal, Rebecca stood alone at the rail of the promenade deck, gazing out over the gently heaving sea. Far to the southeast, she noticed the stars seemed to wink out, as though lost behind some large headland, looming black against the frosty light from the skies.

"Barometer's droppin' like a sounding lead," she heard an officer inform the captain on the bridge above. It had no meaning to her, though the captain's words caused her some concern.

"Muster the deck watch and have them batten down the hatches. Could be we're in for a blow."

Twenty minutes went by with more of the sky blotted out by a swarming inkiness that Rebecca could not discern as roiling clouds. On the main deck, mallets thudded as deck hands stretched watertight canvas over the hatch combings and fitted them in place with wooden wedges. The ship had begun to toss now, the seas running rough, with high waves, crested with foamy spume. Another figure appeared on the deck, stocky and nearly invisible in a dark suit. The man sniffed the air and turned about, eyeing the approaching clouds. Rebecca stepped over to him.

"Excuse me. Mister Riggs is it?"

"Johnathan Riggs, Miss, at your service."

"I'm Rebecca Caldwell. Do you happen to know what is going on?" Rebecca felt a slight queasiness in her stomach, brought on by the violent motion of the ship.

"'Urricane, I'd wager, Miss Caldwell. Or close to it. Seen 'em before, at sea. Ferocious they are." He ran a hand through his thinning black hair and again sniffed the breeze.

"Some sort of storm?"

"The worst sort. Great, twistin' piles of clouds, rain, wind so high it can suck the breath right out of you."

"Like a tornado, then?" Rebecca suggested.

"I'm not acquainted with tornadoes, Miss, but a 'urricane is a big, wide storm front, cover a hundred miles or so, some do."

"But you've been through them before? At sea you said? What was it like?"

"Frightening, to be truthful. I was only a wee bit of a lad, then. Back in the old *HRMS Styraphon*. She was a seventy-four. A big rater even for these modern times. I was a ship's boy. A powder monkey. We had one of them come up off Nassau one time. Blew the squadron to every part of the compass. Swamped a frigate and nearly done for us, too. The commodore, Lord Southington, had his flag aboard *Styraphon*. He had everyone tie on a safety line. We had two boys and an able seaman washed over the side, but the lines saved 'em. We hauled their sodden bodies back aboard each time. We'd trimmed down to nothing but stuns'ls and the main foretop and weathered it out all right. After that, we sailed on the Crimea."

"Lord . . . Southington?"

"Oh, my pardon, miss. Not his present Lordship.

Oh, no. His grandfather. In the fighting with the czar's men, we captured some big Russian prizes, enough to make the fortune of every man and boy aboard."

"Then . . . I hope I'm not being rude, how did you . . . ?"

"Come to be in service, so to speak? Well, I used my share of the prize money to improve my station in life. Went to this school to become a gentleman's gentleman. Learned how to speak properly and to do for my gentleman. The old commodore took me on as a personal aide, first, then after he retired, I went to do for his son. Been with the family ever since."

"That's most interesting, Mr. Riggs."

"Please, miss, Riggs will do," the valet interrupted.

"Ah, Riggs, how will this ship fare in such a storm?"

Riggs studied on the matter a moment. "She's broad of beam. Should help if the draft's enough and the skipper keeps her nose into the storm. It will probably delay our landing at Galveston by somewhat, though."

"Oh, that's too bad. I . . ."

The wind increased suddenly and the temperature plummeted. Raindrops spattered on the deck. Riggs took Rebecca's arm to steady her.

"Best go inside, now, miss. Things will only get worse from here on."

Within a half-hour, a fierce tropical storm battered the ship. *La Belle Marie* wallowed and slammed over the waves, rolling severely from starboard to port as the tempest sledgehammered the vessel. The engines labored mightily against the forces of wind and water. Many of the passengers became seasick, among them Lady Priscilla Parrish. Her *mal de mer* did not decrease her petulant commands, Rebecca discovered when called on to assist with the distressed people.

"It is absolutely obscene," Priscilla complained while Rebecca wiped her face and removed a bowl of

45

slimy bile the afflicted woman had expelled. "How any woman could endure such abominable conditions. Of course, you no doubt have the constitution of a bullock. Peasant stock and all."

"You should really try to eat something," Rebecca suggested. "Perhaps some ship's biscuit. It's what the doctor recommended. Help hold your stomach down."

"Don't you dare mention my internals," Priscilla demanded, gone suddenly green around the mouth. She clutched at her mid-section and bent over. Rebecca barely reached her in time with the basin. "Oh . . ." Lady Priscilla wailed. "Oh, God, I think I am going to die."

"No you won't. Here. Do try to chew this up. There are others I must see to. I'll leave you a cold towel and a fresh basin."

"You'll do nothing of the kind, young woman. I demand that you remain here and tend to my needs."

"Sorry. Captain's orders. There are only a few of us unaffected and we have to spread ourselves thin. Besides, Lady Priscilla, you have a maid to attend you."

"Effie? Lord knows, she will be twice as sick as I."

"All the more reason she needs a woman's comfort. That's where I'm going from here."

"To . . . to care for a *servant*, while I lie here prostrate and wracked with agony? How dare you. It's . . . it's barbaric."

Rebecca had heard all she wanted from this delicate flower and taken more abuse than she believed herself capable of. Her eyes hardened and she started for the door.

"Call it what you want. I lived with the Sioux for five years and I think I know better than you what 'barbaric' is. I'll return after the other ladies aboard are tended to."

"Come back!" Lady Priscilla shrieked at empty space and a closed door.

"This seems to have been going on for days," Jason Plumm remarked to Rebecca an hour later as they paused for coffee in the galley.

"I know. You have certainly been a mainstay to the other passengers, Lord Southington."

"Call me Jason," the young nobleman said through a smile. "And I'll call you Rebecca. It grieves me that you have to put up with Priss' saucy temper."

Rebecca smiled back at his sudden frown. "It's not so bad, once you get the knack of not listening to anything she says."

They laughed together.

"I must admit that Priscilla Parrish is a burden I am content not to have to endure," Jason told her. "I feel a bit sorry for old Tony."

The door burst open and the purser's assistant stood there, sodden from the blinding downpour and tons of sea that washed over the bow. "Can you come at once? We've a crewman with a broken arm and the doctor says he needs assistance."

"We'll be right there," Jason answered. He took Rebecca's cup and his own to a wooden wash tub.

The crewman had been caught by a flying spanner in the engine room. He had been tended by the doctor, who decided the victim needed a better resting place than his bunk in the crew's quarters.

"Take him to my nephew's cabin," Jason offered. "There's a spare bunk he can use."

In the boy's room, Rebecca lighted a gimbaled oil lamp while the men put the seaman on the upper bunk. Christopher looked pale and drawn, his eyes liquid pools of a strange greenish hue with flecks of brown. He raised his head feebly and appealed to Jason.

"Uncle Jason, I feel awful."

"Take it easy, Chris. This will be over soon and you can tell all your friends at Longworth about how you went through a hurricane."

Christopher produced a weak smile. "I really would have rather not had *that* tale to relate, if you don't mind."

Jason smiled at him and ruffled the boy's hair. "That's my boy. Stiff upper and all that. You get some sleep and by morning we'll have blue skies and smooth sailing."

Jason's prediction did not quite come about. The tropical storm roared about the ship at dawn, a murky advent with little light and less promise. A cold breakfast was prepared for those who could eat and, staggering from weariness, Rebecca helped serve it. Lone Wolf had also been stricken by seasickness and she brought him his portion last.

"I am a mess," he protested as she entered his cabin.

"You look it. I brought some biscuit and rice pudding. Do you think you can get it down?"

"No problem on that. It's keeping it there that bothers me. I'd rather have some dried buffalo. That would stop my stomach from jumping and rolling. How is it out there?"

"Not a lot better. Nearly all the British are down sick. Except for Jason. He's been helping. We've been up all night."

"So it's Jason now. That's rather fast." At Rebecca's scowl, he hurried on. "I know he's been a lot of help. He was in twice to see me. It's lucky that some of you were able to stay upright. Man wasn't meant to live on the sea. I'll be glad when this trip is over."

"So will I. Then I can get some sleep."

By eleven the winds had abated and the sun came through the clouds. A long, expectant hour went by until the noon sighting could be made. One by one the afflicted recovered and hastened out to take fresh air on the promenade deck. All except poor, timid Effie. Lady Priscilla loudly demanded her presence to mop the noble brow and fan fresh breezes from the open port across her mistress as Priscilla lay prostrate and complaining. At last the results were made known to the passengers.

"We were blown a long ways off course," the purser announced to those present in the salon. "Even under full power, we won't make port in Galveston until some time tomorrow morning."

"Another night on this wretched hulk," Lady Priscilla complained as she stomped out, beckoning Effie to follow her.

After the meeting broke up, Rebecca stood beside Jason at the rail. In the far distance, the towering clouds of the departing storm provided a dramatic backdrop to the placid contradiction of the swells that ran along with the ship. Rebecca let a few moments of silence pass before she sighed and spoke to Jason.

"I feel all crusty from the salt. I'd certainly like to have a fresh water stream to wash off in."

"I know the feeling. It so happens I have what the ship's brochure refers to as 'a bathing facility' in my cabin. Would you like to avail yourself of it?"

"Oh, I'd . . . love to."

"Be my guest. I'll escort you there and summon hot water."

"It'll be delightful."

Once in his cabin, while they waited for buckets of

49

boiling water to arrive, Jason removed his jacket and went to a sideboard. "A little claret? Or perhaps some sherry. I have Dry Sack and a bit of Fino."

"The sherry would be fine," Rebecca told him. With each second, she was becoming more aware of a deep undercurrent of virile strength in this serious young man. A warmth began to build in her vitals and a glow spread from her loins. For his own part, Rebecca noticed, he seemed acutely aware of her as a woman. Jason poured the drinks and brought her a slender glass of pale amber fluid. He raised his in salute.

"To your very good health."

"And to yours, Jason."

They drank and looked long into each other's eyes. Abruptly Jason broke away and worked on refills. When he returned to her side, he had an air of hesitation about him.

"I . . . I've been inundated with paper work for so long, or off tramping the wilds, so that I'd almost forgotten how . . . how beautiful a woman could be."

"Why, thank you, kind sir."

"No, no. I mean that, Rebecca. You see, I have . . . ah, certain obligations. Affairs pertaining to my land and people, taxes, that sort of thing. And then, I love hunting and exploring strange places. When I'm not compelled to the one, I'm indulging in the other. It doesn't leave much time for, ah, for the tender pursuits. Then, when confronted by such an attractive and warm person as yourself, I hardly know what to say, where to begin."

"If what you want to say is that you find me attractive, I must tell you that the feeling is mutual. As to where to begin, might I suggest you kiss me?"

Jason reached for her when a knock came at the door.

"Bath water," a boy's voice piped through the panel.

"Br-er, bring it in," Jason commanded.

When the boy had poured, been tipped and departed, Jason took Rebecca into his arms. "Now, where were we?"

"You were going to kiss me."

"And then?"

"Then . . ." Rebecca looked around the cabin and her eyes glowed with mischief at the sight of rising clouds of steam. "Then why don't you join me in that tub?"

They undressed silently and in a rush. As Rebecca suspected, Jason's body was pale, rarely ever exposed to the sun, and he had a bit of softness around his middle. The muscles above, in arms and shoulders, were hard enough, though, and his rapidly elongating penis soon would be.

With equal excitement and interest, Jason examined her. He had never seen such a glowing, coppery complexion before. Her breasts, large and firm, stood pertly, almost virginal, on her chest and the silken flesh arrowed down to a delightfully narrow waist and lusciously flaring hips. She had hardly any pubic hair on her puffily swollen mound, as opposed to the luxurious tufts of dark auburn threads that sprouted from the thick base of his up-curved manhood. He gave her a quick, slightly nervous smile and stepped close.

Rebecca came into his arms and clung with her body firmly against his so that his throbbing maleness pressed urgently against her taut belly. They kissed again. Sometime, during the long osculation, though Jason was not fully aware when, Rebecca's hand began to steal down his knobby frame until she grasped his aching phallus and began to bring it relief. When they parted, she kept hold of his abundant maleness and directed him toward the tub.

"You get in first. Then I'll join you."

Jason obeyed, some three inches of his raging steed protruding above water level. A delighted smile made Rebecca's face angelically radiant as she stepped into the hot bath and lowered herself seductively toward the pulsing object of her most sincere affection. With one hand she guided it to her moist and slippery purse, while the other held her poised in place above the entranced young man. Slowly she prepared him with her wetness, and Jason moaned at the delicious sensations of that tender touch. Then Rebecca lowered herself until she had ingested all that stuck above the surface.

"Aaah," Jason sighed and shuddered through his considerable length. "More. Take me in deeper."

Rebecca shook her head. "Not yet. Let me soap your chest while we get to know each other better."

She controlled her position with her knees while she administered a thick lather to Jason's hairless chest. All the while, magic muscles, the function of which had never been known to Jason before, massaged and kneaded his throbbing phallus in a manner wholly delightful and utterly new to him.

"Oh, that's so good," he gasped.

"You don't have any idea how wonderful it is to me, sweet Jason," Rebecca cooed. "I could go on like this all day."

"You'd . . . you'd drive me mad," Jason declared with a grunt as he tried to thrust himself upward into her. Water slopped over the sides of the copper tub.

"See what you've done, you naughty boy."

Rebecca lowered herself another inch and they both sighed their contentment. She began to rock her hips from side to side. Jason slid his lance backward, then drove suddenly into her honeyed channel, only to be stopped at the same four inch mark by tightly constricted muscles.

"Oh . . . my . . . God . . . this is unbearable."

"Yes, Jason, yes. It's called the honey torture."

Accustomed to the delightful game, Jason withdrew nearly to the end of his dark red tip, then thrust forward and swayed with the gyrations of her hips.

"That's an odd name. Where did you learn to do it?" he inquired in gasps as they gleefully repeated the procedure twice more.

"In the swimming hole of a creek outside an Oglala village. It was the summer I turned sixteen. A boy named Four Horns taught me."

"An aborigine?" Jason exploded. He nearly lost the keen edge of his erection.

"Yes. I'm half Sioux, myself," Rebecca replied as she relaxed those mystifying muscular rings and plunged down on Jason's last five inches. She shuddered with tingling pleasure at the welcome fullness of him so deep within her sensitive, pulsating passage and threw back her head.

"Now, Jason," she pleaded. "Now. Love me with all your might!"

FIVE

"Stop it! Do you want to snatch me bald?" Lady Priscilla Parrish yelled at her maid as the girl ran a comb through the noblewoman's hair.

"B-b-but, ma'am, I was only trying to comb out your lovely hair." Tears formed in Effie's eyes at the venomous tone of her mistress.

"Leave it be and get out of here, you stupid cow!" Effie fled, a hand to her mouth to stifle her sobs.

"I say," Lord Anthony Parrish drawled. "You're being rather harsh with the poor girl, aren't you?"

"Don't you start, too, Tony. Since Jason has taken up with that common baggage, I've had all I can do to prevent an outbreak of utter insolence among the servants. For the life of me, I wish we had never come to this dreadful country."

"The storm has left you overwrought, my dear. I'll see if I can fetch up a cup of tea."

Priscilla took a deep breath and looked at her pinched, angry face in the mirror. Wouldn't do, she thought, to let too much show. "Yes. That would be nice. Make sure that dolt of a cook takes the pot to the water, not the other way around, as the Americans are wont to do."

Anthony departed and Priscilla began to stalk the cabin floor. How, oh, how had that American trollop captured Jason's attentions? She looked . . . oriental, only a hint, but it was there. Imagine, living among the savages for five years. The girl had told her that, she recalled, despite her wretched condition during the storm. Well, she had heard stories of what the aborigines did to captive white women. She doesn't seem any the worse for her ordeal, Priscilla considered furiously. Perhaps she enjoyed it.

Simmering frustration came to a boil in her breast. They had made love. Of that she was sure. One could tell those things. The satisfied smirk on Jason's lips. The girl's brazen strut and bold eyes on him. Why could it not have been . . . Her thoughts broke off, one part of her afraid to give life to what the other desired.

She had wanted children when she married Anthony Parrish ten years ago. Somehow they had never been blessed. The onus, of course, fell on her. Tradition dictated that it had to be she who was barren. For five years it had been a constant agony for her. Then something happened inside her. She and Anthony had drifted apart, though they remained together. Her self-recriminations ceased and her affection for Tony dried up.

For his own part, he affected not to notice. The management of his estates seemed to occupy all his time. Talking cows and sheep, cheeses and onions with stolid farmers in dung-smeared boots apparently delighted Anthony. As did setting right the grievances of his tenants. Be they husbandmen, tradesmen, or foresters, they enjoyed more license and favor with

Lord Anthony Parrish than any other common herd in all of England. As the gulf between her and her husband widened, Priscilla began to resent this liberal attitude on Anthony's part. What right had he to make reforms that threatened the very structure of British society, and in process made her look equally ridiculous in the eyes of their peers? It was so . . . so *déclassé*. Priscilla started, a physical flinching of her body, when the cabin door opened and Anthony entered with a tray.

A silver tea service gleamed on it, matching the hearty smile on his wide face. He set it on the sideboard and poured. Before serving, he removed his monocle from his left eye and wiped it industriously with his pocket kerchief. The nervous habit had come to irritate Priscilla worse than a brazen snore did other women.

"There now," Lord Anthony soothed. "A stout cup will do you worlds of good."

Crisp sheets rustled as the two young lovers moved against each other. The rigid shaft churning deep inside her sent shivers of delight tingling through Rebecca's body. Slowly, ever so slowly, she and Jason continued the dance of love. She had never expected a sea voyage to be quite so exciting. The reflection brought a low murmur trembling up through her throat.

"Making love in the afternoon is quite new to me," Jason observed.

"To me, also," Rebecca agreed. It took a conscious effort to keep from telling him that she had begun the practice six weeks earlier. The acknowledgement sent a pang of guilt through her. Had she truly loved Philipe? Was her current affair an indication she was a wanton woman? Try as she might, she could not feel deep remorse.

She needed love as greatly as any man. That much she had come to terms with long before her body had experienced it.

Desire burned with the same hot flame within her as in any lusty male. Most women, she knew, denied this and constantly suppressed their natural needs. Under instruction from mothers over eons past, and supported by the doctrine of most religions, they learned to purge their bodies of any pleasurable sensations connected with the act. Sex was supposed to be the price they paid for a home and the security of a husband. For a woman, the carnal joys were expected to be dry and painful experiences, indulged in only on the brutish demand of their mate and for the exclusive purpose of procreation. To hell with that, Rebecca thought as she felt herself floating deliciously upward to the peak. To reject her nature was to reject herself. When love, real, enduring love, came along, she would know. For now she let go all bonds and immersed herself in the most wonderful of sensations.

Shrill whistles throughout the harbor and a brass band met *La Belle Marie* when the side-wheeler steamed into Galveston, Texas, somewhat battered but undaunted, by the storm. Captains of other vessels called greetings over their brass megaphones, which the master of the packet returned goodnaturedly.

"We thought you'd been lost with all hands," one exclaimed. "God's mercy that you made it."

"Welcome, Hiram," another hollered. "Ye look funny with that stack stoved in. Run into a granite cloud, did ye?"

"No harder than your head, O'Brien," the steam

packet's skipper bantered back.

Docking took a long fifteen minutes before the gangplank swung outboard and lowered to the thick planks. Passengers began to disembark. Rebecca and Lone Wolf went first to check on their horses.

"Look, Ike caught a bad scrape in the storm," Rebecca advised, pointing to a spot on the big Morgan's left hindquarter. "I didn't see that the first time."

"We had some rough seas after the hurricane, too," Lone Wolf reminded her. "We had better check on unloading them."

"Right. And I hope there is rail transportation available most of the way. Texas is big. We could spend months traveling around until we found Tulley."

Their preparations caused them to be last to leave the ship. Jason Plumm waited at the bottom of the gangplank. He removed his short crown beaver hat and twisted it in his blunt fingers.

"I, ah, wanted to ask you an enormous favor. The both of you."

"What is that, Jason?" Rebecca inquired sweetly.

"Well, the simple matter is . . . you see . . . you and Mister Baylor here know a great deal more about your country than we do. If it isn't asking too much, I . . . we would appreciate it if you advised us on outfitting for our hunting expedition. Our wagons will not be off-loaded until tomorrow, so there is plenty of time."

"Why, we would be delighted to help you, Jason. Wouldn't we?" Rebecca gave Lone Wolf a nudge.

"Uh . . . yeah. Sure we would."

"Right off hand we'll need a good outfitter here in Galveston."

"You're going northwest, from what Rebecca has told me, toward the Panhandle? Is that right?"

"Yes. So we'll need plenty of provisions, proper

camp equipment, all that sort of thing."

"Why not wait until you get further on? Take the train to Austin, or even beyond that?"

"Really, Mr. Baylor, I hadn't given the matter any thought."

"Moving by wagon and pack-train is slow. This is a large state. You could spend weeks between here and any prime hunting country. And, call me, ah, Bret."

"Certainly, Bret, and I'm Jason. I have a second invitation to offer. It would please me greatly if you two would consent to join our expedition. At least until you reach your own destination. We'll have a jolly good time. Monson's a first-rate cook and I made arrangements for a wide selection of excellent wines."

"Sounds delightful," Lone Wolf said dryly. Rebecca wanted to kick him in the shin. "We'll consider that. In the meanwhile, why not see to your wagons, arrange for them to be put on a train car, and we can oversee outfitting your party when we get to Austin."

"Capital. Capital. I want to thank you both. Also to urge you to accept the invitation to come along. Good day, now."

Rebecca steamed in silence. Always, Lone Wolf had deferred to her wishes and plans in their quest for vengeance against the Tulley gang and Roger Styles. Now he and, even more irritatingly, Jason talked around her. Why, they had relegated her to the role of most women, whether in white or Indian society. *They* were making the decisions. *They* laid plans and only passingly included her in the conversation. Well, *they* had a surprise coming.

The locomotive was noisy, dirty, and a decade out of date. It sent showers of cinders and coal dust floating back over the cars, coating everything with grime. It reminded Rebecca of one that the Oglala band of Iron Calf had decided to attack early in the long years of her captivity. . . .

. . . "The white-eyes have brought the iron road to our land and it is a bad thing," one of Iron Calf's principal warriors had spoken in counsel. "We must drive it away. In a dream I saw us attacking the snorting demon that pulls the *wasicun* in their boxes. We put arrows into it and the iron horse hissed white vapor at us. More arrows and more. Then it began to slow. Its hot, smoking blood ran out and it grew weak. Like a big bull buffalo, it at last had to stop. Then we swarmed over it and killed all the evil whites. I have spoken."

Fat Antelope's words had been electric, Rebecca recalled. A war party had been hastily organized and the men rode off to the railroad. A large number of women, including herself, trailed along behind to watch the fun.

Late the next day, a locomotive pulling ten cars came puffing along the track. At a signal from Fat Antelope, the warriors charged, firing arrows into the sides of the locomotive.

Most bounced off. Several, though, pierced the age-weakened sides of the big mushroom-stacked engine. Steam shrieked out from the wounds. Encouraged, the Oglala charged again. More arrows pierced the mighty vehicle. One brave drove his lance into the wooden side of the first car behind the tender. He neglected to let go and the train's momentum yanked him from his saddle and deposited him, screaming in horror, under the wheels of the cattle car.

Once again, the warriors made an assault. Rifle fire answered them from the passenger cars and the mail coach. Two more braves died. The locomotive chugged and hissed its way along the rails. Another warrior shrieked and spun off his pony, raising dust when he hit the ground. In a frantic effort to fulfil his dream, Fat Antelope fired an entire magazine through his repeater, piercing the boiler at several points. A Winchester slammed from an open window and yet another Oglala clutched at his chest and slipped off the side of his mount. The big Baldwin slowed imperceptibly. Before the advantage could be tipped toward the shouting Indians, the war ponies began to tire, low on stamina from a diet of only grass.

Frustrated, Fat Antelope raced after the dwindling target and hurled his lance at the rear in a final show of defiance. Its long, sharp blade pierced the door of the caboose and the conductor standing behind it. Then, with an obscene gesture, Fat Antelope led the warriors away in a wide sweep across the prairie.

There had been much mourning in the village for the five dead warriors. Rebecca wondered afterward that if she had been brave enough to dash down to the train and leap aboard, she might have escaped her life of drudgery in Iron Calf's village. Although unfulfilled, it was a hope to cling to. . . .

. . . Some gigantic jackrabbits bounded away from the train and Chris Anderson shouted with excitement, drawing Rebecca from her reverie.

"Can I pot one of them from the vestibule, Uncle Jason?"

"No, Chris. We shoot only what we want to eat or for trophies. Besides, the rifles are with our baggage up forward. You could never get to one in time. They're only common hares, though rather large, I must say."

"Jackrabbits," Lone Wolf informed him.

Even on the train, Rebecca's status had been relegated to that of any other woman of the times. She had been seated with Lady Priscilla and was expected, she supposed, to confine her conversation to womanly topics. So far, they had only exchanged icy glances. The woman hated her, Rebecca knew that much, though she had no idea why.

"During the storm, you mentioned that you had been a captive of the savages," Lady Priscilla began, opening a conversation that, while it offended her to have to, she hoped would provide her with something to drive a wedge between the brazen hussy and Jason Plumm. "Tell me about it, if it's not too distressing."

"Where should I start? With Bitter Creek Jake Tulley and my low-life uncles trading my mother and me off to Iron Calf's Oglala Sioux in exchange for their own rotten lives? Or how I was beaten and kicked about and made to do the filthiest sort of work in the camp?" Inwardly, Rebecca relished it when the noble Briton displayed an expression of utter disgust. "Would you like to hear about my husband and my baby? I was sixteen and he two years older the first time we made . . . uh, became intimate. We were not married then. He came to me while I was bathing in a stream. He removed his clothes and dived into the water and we . . . we began fumbling around like young people do. That night he slipped into my mother's lodge by crawling under a side skirt that I had loosened and we made love."

"My word!" Priscilla exploded despite herself.

"Yes, it was exciting. His name was Four Horns and to a girl who had never experienced anything like that before, it felt like he had all four before the night was over. We had a son. Four Horns and our baby were killed in a raid by the Crow." She noted Priscilla's startled, doubting look and hurried on.

"Oh, I know, it has become popular in certain intellectual circles to pretend that the Indians were peace-loving children of nature before the white man came. 'Lo, the noble savage . . .'" she quoted. "Well, *Lo* never existed, I can assure you. The popular myth has it that there had never been any warfare, any killing, scalping or torture, until the wicked Europeans taught these things to the innocent savages. Believe me, more Indians have died, and are still dying, at the hands of other Indians, than all those killed by whites.

"Their living conditions are squalid at best, their habits barbaric, and the torments they inflict on enemies and captives are monstrous. I have that on the best of authority, considering that I am half Sioux."

"My good Lord!" Lady Priscilla had become pale, then furious red and pale again as Rebecca regaled her with her tale. Now she put a hand to her breast, as though personally threatened.

"They have religion, you know. And a code of ethics. They respect the property of another, but disdain ownership for their own pleasure. The biggest man in the tribe is the one who gives away the most of what he owns."

"Dear me. Please, please, spare me any more of these . . . these fanciful exploits. It quite disturbs my constitution."

"Life is hard out here, Lady Priscilla. I sought to let you understand how only the strongest survive," she concluded in a thinly veiled threat.

Rebecca sat back with a private smile. She was supposed to keep her place with the women, chatter with Lady Priscilla, let the men decide things. That seemed to be the plan. She had tried that . . . and gained a lot of satisfaction from the effort. But Jake Tulley lurked out there somewhere and when the time came to go after him, it would be she who gave the orders. Wait until Austin, or beyond it, my two fine male friends, she thought with satisfaction, and we'll see who shows what to whom.

SIX

A meadowlark gave an experimental sunrise trill that set off responses from the golden breast of an amorous fellow. In turn that brought forth the spritely call of quail and sorrowful clarion of mourning doves. Simon Weissman scratched at the fringe of graying black hair that edged his bald pate and poured himself a cup of coffee. He yawned, stretched, and shuffled to the counter that held his telegraph key and sounder. With a practiced hand, he struck the spring-loaded device and sent the signal down the wire that Bascomb, Texas was open for traffic.

Two seconds later, the response came back from the Lubbock operator. Simon nodded wisely and raised his cup to his lips. Suddenly he halted. Had he seen a movement out in the high grass north of town?

What it was, he couldn't tell. Darkness still cloaked much of the prairie and his eyes weren't what they used to be. He squinted and fumbled on his gold-rimmed spectacles. There. It came again. Clearer now. Riders.

A lot of them.

"Oy veh!" he gasped aloud when he recognized the forms. "Comanches." His hand went automatically to the key. While he studied the approaching marauders, he sent word along the line in dots and dashes.

"Bascomb, number seven-nine, unknown number of hostiles approaching town in stealth, send help, send help, will keep sending as long . . ." the line went dead. Cut, Simon figured, by the Indians.

The Comanches had grown closer now and among them Simon recognized the clothing and postures of white men. Captives? No. Not when they carried rifles in their arms. Simon reached into a drawer and took out an old Hopkins and Allan revolver. He checked that the cylinder moved freely and added some loose cartridges to the pocket of his tan sweater. Then he rose and walked purposefully to the door.

No doubt about it. Comanches. Simon's heart pounded in his frail chest. The town had to be warned. That would rob the hostiles of their surprise. Only one way he could do anything. He raised the old revolver and took careful aim on the chest of the nearest warrior. He held his breath a moment and fired.

Opie Dillon heard a meaty smack to the left of him, followed almost instantly by the crack of a shot. The stocky, muscular Comanche beside him showed an expression of utter surprise and his head drooped so that he looked at the hole in his chest. He uttered a soft sigh and slipped from his pony's back. Opie glanced forward.

A short, balding man stood at the door to the telegraph office, a billow of greasy smoke powder blowing away from him. A yellow flash appeared at the end of his extended arms, and Opie heard the bullet sizzle through the air close to his head.

"Indians! Indians!" a distant voice called. "Everyone take cover. Comanches coming!"

That wouldn't do, Opie thought, as he unlimbered the Winchester in the crook of his left elbow. Before he could take aim, the church bell began to ring. Then came the strident clang of a triangle outside the firehouse. Opie leveled his rifle and sighted on the small man's chest.

The steel butt-plate slammed Opie's shoulder. A brisk morning breeze blew away the smoke powder and he saw the bullet impact in the little man's stomach. The telegrapher staggered back, raised his revolver again and fired. Another Comanche went off to the Great Spirit before Opie triggered his second shot.

This time he saw a spray of blood and brains as the little man slammed backward into the doorjamb, hit square between the eyes. Opie stood in the stirrups and waved his Winchester over his head.

"Let's get 'em!" he called.

"What the hell!" Grant Williams, marshal of Bascomb, came out of a sound sleep talking aloud. The church bell and fire alarm clamored outside the jail and he wondered if there was a fire. He strapped on his gunbelt and dashed for the door.

At the far end of Main Street, he saw galloping riders pounding into town. His first thought was that a trail herd had camped nearby and the drovers had been let loose for a final fling before heading north to Kansas. But that made no sense. This was late fall. Then he saw, riding with the white men, half a dozen Comanche braves. By God, it was a raid.

Williams dodged back into the office, secured a rifle from the wall rack and hurried to the plankwalk that fronted the stone-walled jail and office. He raised the weapon to his shoulder and took quick aim on the nearest hostile.

A powerful blast from the .44 Winchester cleaned one Comanche out of his saddle. He hurtled through the air and snapped his spine on a tie-rail. Quickly the marshal sighted on a scruffy-looking white renegade and let go another round.

The Tulley gang became a member short when Williams' 205 grain slug smashed into the outlaw's chest, clipped shards off two ribs, and burst his heart. He continued to ride, tall in the saddle, for ten fast strides of his mount before he pitched forward, slipped around the side of his wall-eyed horse's neck and dropped under the plunging hoofs. By then the street swarmed with raiders. Grant Williams jumped back inside the office and dropped the bar in place. He continued to fire through a slotted opening in the door.

His next bullet cracked into the eyesocket of a Comanche pony and sent its rider sprawling in the dust, large patches of skin peeling from his cheeks and nose. Before the warrior could recover, a load of buckshot from the doorway of the mercantile turned his back into gory sausage. A momentary lull came in the fighting. Williams heard a slight noise behind him and, thinking of his two prisoners, a drunk and a petty thief, he turned to investigate.

Sonney Boyle peered into the jail through a small, barred window set in the stone rear wall. He saw the figure of the marshal appear in the interconnecting doorway and start down past the tier of four cells. At that moment, the marshal saw him.

"Hey, you. At the back of the jail. Ride to get help. We can hold these heathens for a while. Hurry, man!"

A beatific grin spread on Sonney Boyle's face. He raised his Colt and eared back the hammer. The bullet sped from its muzzle and struck Grant Williams in the stomach.

The marshal tried to bring his own weapon into play but a second loud crash came from Boyle's six-gun and a terrible pain blossomed in the marshal's chest. He staggered backward and slid down the wall that framed the door. A wide smear of blood brightened the drab buff paint.

"Wha'zat?" the drunk muttered, dragged out of his stupor by the sound of shots. He looked up in time to see a yellow-orange flower blossom at the end of Sonney's Colt. Then a blackness, more profound and prolonged than any brought on by liquor, enveloped him.

"No, mister! Please!" the sneak-thief shrieked. "I'm on'y sixteen."

"You'll not make seventeen," Boyle advised him a moment before he put a slug in the kid's chest.

With a high, ululating whoop, *Osolo* galloped down the center of a residential street that paralleled Main. He fired at the backs of white children who ran in terror for shelter in root cellars and houses.

The whirring shafts struck one child after another, sent them sprawling and kicking out their lives in front of their horrified parents. Big Wolf swelled his chest with pride. He knew himself to be the best in Rolling Thunder's band when it came to rapid fire of arrows from horseback. He rarely missed. Others praised him, too, so he felt confident in claiming the honor. He nocked another missile and took aim on a tow-headed boy who scrambled to get over the lip of a cellar door.

With a wicked slap, the shaft drove deep into the youngster's back and the flint point protruded from his belly, dripping gore. *Osolo* wheeled his mount to the left then and charged toward the center of town. Many more whites waited to die.

Methodically, Lou Nettles loaded and fired his big Sharps rifle from inside his general mercantile. The heavy detonations reverberated off the walls and ceiling and made a flat crack from the face of buildings across the street. Sudden motion to his left swung the fifty-caliber weapon that direction and Lou fired instinctively.

A painted Comanche flew from the back of his pony as though on springs. Lou reloaded and took closer aim at the next to ride past, a smoking revolver in his hand.

Instantly, Lou took pressure off the trigger. A white man. Certain the stranger had to be on his side, the merchant hurried to the door.

"Hey. In here. They'll cut you to pieces out there."

The white man reined in and swung from the saddle. He strode quickly to the boardwalk and into the store. Then he removed his bowler hat with his left hand in a gesture of gratitude.

"Much obliged," a grinning Jake Tulley told Lou Nettles a fraction of a second before he gunned the mercantile dealer down.

*   *   *

70

Instantly, Jake went to the dead man's side and rifled his pockets for valuables and cash. He took what he found and hurried to the counter.

A bell jangled when Jake opened the cash drawer. He scooped out paper money and all the coin he could locate. He knew there had to be a better cache somewhere. Bascomb did not have a bank.

Flour made a white haze in the air as Jake began to ransack the shelves, looking for a secret panel that would reveal the merchant's horde of money. He hurled bolts of cloth off onto the floor, to mingle with spilled brine from the pickle barrel and gooey molasses from a broken keg. Rice and beans made brittle sounds as they bounced off the walls in showers of grain. Still the expected bankroll did not appear.

As he worked, Jake also dumped boxes of ammunition into a flour sack and added items of value when he encountered them. So intent was he on his quest that he failed to hear soft footsteps at the top of a flight of stairs that led to the second floor living quarters.

Judith Nettles, Lou's wife, stood there a moment, eyes round and white at the horror of her beloved's corpse, then she turned her attention to the intruder. Slowly she raised the twin barrels of a sawed-off Parker and centered the front brass bead on Tulley's back. Her hands trembled and she fought tears as she eared back a hammer and squeezed the trigger.

Tulley heard the metallic ratcheting of the shotgun hammer and instinctively dived for cover. A shattering boom came from above and a load of buckshot smashed into the counter over his head. Not all of the pellets went stray, though. Jake cringed from the stinging, numbing pain in his left shoulder, caused by three lead balls. Instantly furious, he rose and whipped his six-gun in line with the attractive young woman at the head of the stairs.

Judith Nettles didn't hear the sound of the shot that sent a bullet smashing into her throat. It ripped through her carotid artery and exited in a welter of blood and fluid alongside her spine.

Heels drumming into his pony's flanks, *Osolo* rounded into Main Street. He reined in his pony in front of a large building. Although he had no knowledge of the words, a large sign declared it to be the hotel. He saw several of the white renegades inside, gathering the yellow-metal objects, so he turned his mount's head to the left and started off. At that moment, a young woman came out of the alley.

Images of tender, alabaster flesh, flailing legs, and a hot, slippery passage into which he plunged his raging manhood filled Big Wolf's head. He leered at the gaping woman and lunged his horse forward, a fiery swelling in his loins pushing out the hem of his Comanche hunting shirt.

The woman, he saw, raised both of her arms and he caught the glare of sunlight off metal. She held herself rigid as he rode down on her. Then, in a flash of frightful clarity, he recognized the object she held. He started to throw himself aside as a fat fireball formed at the muzzle of the old Confederate Starr .44.

Heated by blast and friction, the heavy round ball produced a popping sound when it slammed into *Osolo's* forehead. The soft lead flattened out on his skull and pushed a large plug of bone ahead of it as it ripped into his brain. His erection withered to a tiny lump and the hot piece of metal erased all thoughts of lust.

With a grunt, the Comanche warrior, best bowman of the band, flipped over backward and hit the street with a sodden thump.

Almost instantly, a blood-smeared lance tip burst out through one of the woman's breasts, driven from behind by *Sahonkeno*. Fox spared a brief second to look down at the woman's writhing body before he wrenched his lance free and rode on. Resistance dwindled rapidly. Here and there, Fox heard the screams of women and girls who had been captured and were now being energetically raped by the warriors and their white allies. He turned away and started organizing braves to set fire to all the buildings.

Opie Dillon pulled down the little girl's bloomers and sat her on the edge of a low table. Then he began to fumble with his fly.

Her face a model of wide-eyed innocence, the girl watched what he did and sucked in her breath when he exposed his reddened, throbbing penis. "Are you going to put it in there?" she asked, her voice trembling with anticipation as she pointed to her hairless mound.

"That's right, honey." Opie stepped forward, between legs that she spread wide to receive him.

"Oooh! That tickles," she squealed as he slid his slender shaft into her small opening.

Opie drew back and thrust deeper, accompanied by her cries of delight. His frenzy mounted with each plunge.

"Oh, you're nice . . . real nice," he murmured.

"More!" she demanded, wrapping her slender arms around his wide torso.

Sonney Boyle found them like that. His lips curled in

contempt and he spat on the floor. "You're disgustin', Opie. You know that? Damn down-right disgustin'. She cain't be more'n ten, eleven. It's filthy."

"B-but she likes it, Sonney," Opie protested. "You can be next."

"You oughtta be ashamed of yourself. Both of you." Vexed beyond control, Sonney walked out of the small house and started toward the center of town. He shoulda gunned 'em down. Both of 'em. Sick is what they were.

"There you are, sir," the bustling clerk at the Austin outfitter's shop enthused to Jason Plumm. "All set up. You've five pack saddles, canvas covers, enough rope to secure it all and have some spare. Also all your cooking gear: dutch oven, kettles, skillets, tripod, rotisserie rig, ladles, and the works. Now, as to firearms."

"We have our own, thanks," Jason responded, bringing a slight frown of disappointment to the clerk's forehead. He turned to Lone Wolf.

"Can you think of anything else?"

"Not really. Fact is, I've never traveled with all that much. Now, I think we ought to meet Becky. She's on something."

They found Rebecca where she had told them she was going. A small saloon on the corner had been scandalized when she entered, dressed in proper woman's outfit. Several patrons hastily emptied their glasses and departed. Others remained to gawk and whisper speculations. Rebecca sat at a round deal table with two dark-skinned men. When Lone Wolf and Jason entered, she motioned for them to join her.

"Jason Plumm, Bret Baylor, this is Issac Curleyhead

and Cootyarkey Journeycake. They have agreed to act as guides for your expedition, Jason," Rebecca told him in a tone that brooked no disagreement.

"I, ah, that is, good afternoon, gentlemen. What sort of arrangements have you made on my behalf as regards pay?" Jason asked Rebecca.

"The usual. Dollar a day each and a share of any saleable pelts taken."

"This Bret is the one you call Lone Wolf?" Cootyarkey asked her.

"Yes."

"Lone Wolf?" Jason asked, surprised at this sudden revelation.

"My, ah, name among the Crow. After hearing it for over ten years, it's more comfortable than Bret Baylor," Lone Wolf explained.

"My, my. Then you have both been captive among the sav . . . er, Indians?"

Issac laughed. "No need to be sensitive on our account, Mister Plumm. We Delaware have lived among the whites for so long we think of ourselves as being part of you."

"Thank you, Mister Curleyhead."

"Call me Issac. My family are Christian. I have a son in the Baptist Mission School in Kansas. I have to go this far, sometimes, to find work."

"Ah . . ." Jason cleared his throat. "Shall we all go along to the hotel and meet the others?"

"What about livestock?" Cootyarkey asked.

"Be ready in the morning," Jason informed him. "We can load them on the train and be aboard in time to go to San Angelo. Now, let's be off, shall we?"

"Stone the crows," Riggs exploded in uncharacteristic vulgarity at sight of the two Delaware who entered the large sitting room with his employer, Rebecca, and the man he called Bret. "Bleedin' savages they are."

75

"Riggs!"

"Oh . . . sorry, sir. Won't happen again, sir. Will you be wanting tea, sir?"

"Yes, Riggs. Straightaway if you please. And I suppose our guests would prefer a bit of whiskey?"

"Fine with me," Cootyarkey allowed.

"What is tea?" his companion asked.

Shortly, the rest of the British party arrived. Explanations were made regarding preparations for the journey and the hiring of two guides. That brought the expected objections and counter suggestions from Lady Priscilla. Then Jason exploded another surprise.

"I want again to extend my most sincere invitation for you, Rebecca, and you, ah, Lone Wolf, to accompany us. At least to your own destination."

"What!" Lady Priscilla howled in wounded pride. "I . . . I'll hear of no such a thing."

"It is, after all, Priss, *my* expedition," Jason gently reminded her. "Their experience will be invaluable to us." He turned back to the stalwart pair. "Well, what do you say?"

Rebecca thought of the two shiny-new, totally impractical wagons brought all the way from New Orleans. Spindly-wheeled, thin-sided, and far too fragile to endure long on the rugged prairie, they forecasted disaster. She thought also of the wonderful warmth and release Jason brought to her. A wistful smile graced her lips.

Lone Wolf considered also the equipage, the lack of plains knowledge, and the obvious fact that Jason Plumm and his party would need all the help they could get. He nodded solemnly.

"Yes," Rebecca answered for them both when she saw her companion's silent assent. "We will be glad to accompany you, Jason. First thing in the morning, then?"

76

SEVEN

Suddenly the bunch of brightly colored flowers disappeared right before their eyes!

A ripple of awed surprise ran through the assembled Comanches. Even the mighty *Kansaleumko* lost his impassive expression and registered amazement. Roger Styles smiled at his audience and, in his poor Comanche, began the patter for his next simple stage magician's illusion.

A group of big-eyed boys stood at the rear of the gathering. A tow-headed youngster, Horst Bieleson, among them, dressed only in loincloth and moccasins, his skin just beginning to darken, appeared as breathlessly entranced as the savages. *Kansaleumko*—Rolling Thunder—turned to his second in command, Fox.

"The great *Maman-ti* has long been gone and dead now in that place called Florida," the war chief said quietly. "How is it that this white man has brought such powerful medicine, even more mystifying than that of the Kiowa prophet and medicine man, Sky-Walker?"

"It is a sacred mystery," Fox agreed. "I do not know. *Maman-ti* had been made master over all Kiowa and Comanche medicine men. Yet This One comes with magic that has no equal in all the Sky-Walker taught. When this ends, it will be time," he reminded his leader.

"Yes." Rolling Thunder flashed a grim smile. "Go and make the preparations now."

Roger Styles found himself filled with exhilaration. The raid on Bascomb had gone well. Jake Tulley and his men brought back over seven thousand dollars. An impressive amount. That had been late yesterday afternoon. The war dancing and scalp ceremony went on all night. This morning they had enjoyed a typical Comanche breakfast.

Long strips of horse meat had been broiled over coals on four-foot stakes. Smoking and crisp on the outside, the barely warmed-through flesh had been brought into the lodge Styles shared with Jake Tulley. The women rammed the handle end of each stick into the earth and brought bark dishes of kiln-dried corn that had been boiled to a turn and mashed. They were, Roger discovered with distaste, expected to eat with only their knives and fingers. The savages didn't even provide him with salt or other condiments. Beside him, Jake Tulley had dug in with all the fastidiousness of a pig in a slop trough.

All the same, it proved satisfying. After the meal, Fox came to him and explained that *Kansaleumko* wished Roger to display his powerful medicine for the entire encampment. Roger had readily agreed.

"Cheap magician's tricks," Jake scoffed. "They ever get on to you an' we'll both lose our hair. Whiskey's better with Injuns."

"Don't be a complete ass, Jake. Their primitive minds will never allow them to grasp what it is I am doing. They see it as something mystical, a part of their

78

barbaric religion. They would never dream of looking beyond the physical appearance of magic. Given enough whiskey and they would murder their own mothers. No, this is the best way. Would I lie to you?"

Now, as his performance came to a close, Roger wondered what would be next in store. Beyond the heads of his audience, he saw a cluster of braves around a set of poles driven into the ground. A small fire burned nearby, and the old singers and drummers gathered there while he pulled a small, white dove from inside a battered old top hat. Oohs and ahs rose from the crowd and some of the women clapped their palms against cheeks in a sign of wondrous approval.

"Chemakacho!" the Comanches cried. *"Chemakacho!"*

"Come," Rolling Thunder commanded Roger after the last illusion. "Now we all grow strong from the captives' hearts."

Unaware of what was to happen, Roger and Jake followed as the entire band strolled to the strong, high posts the outlaw leader had seen earlier. Facing each other, two sets had been driven into the ground some three feet apart. Standing between the pairs, Roger recognized Rupert Bieleson and Ab Simmons. The captives from Johnas Point. They had been stripped naked and their arms drawn up as far as they could reach. Their hands were tied to the nearest stake. Their feet had also been bound to the posts near the ground. Behind him, Roger heard a scuffle and a high-pitched voice cried out.

"Papa!" Horst Bieleson shouted. Then a strong hand clapped over his mouth and its owner, a powerful warrior named Big Spotted Cat, lifted the struggling boy off his feet.

Rolling Thunder and a number of his old men stationed themselves near Roger and Tulley. Then the war chief made a signal to the drummers. With Rolling Thunder in the lead, at the head of all his warriors, they moved forward slowly, silently, in a single file. Their pace was a peculiar half walk, half shuffle with a spasmodic, nervous motion to their limbs and torsos. Each carried in one hand his favorite knife or tomahawk, in the other a flint stone, perhaps three to five inches in length, shaped like a sharp-pointed arrowhead.

The head of the procession circled a long way around, so that the file formed a sinuous shape like a crawling snake. Rolling Thunder first approached Rupert Bieleson, then Ab Simmons. As the serpentine line wound past, two of the youngest warriors broke from the parade and seized the pinioned white men by the hair and scalped them, then resumed their places and moved on.

The operation consisted of cutting off only a portion of the skin which covers the skull, in the diameter of a silver dollar. Blood flowed freely from each ravaged head, running down over their faces and trickling from their chins. Up to this time there had been entire silence, except a yell from the two young men when they performed the scalpings and the throb of drums. Now, as the hackles rose on Roger Styles' neck, the whole party halted for thirty seconds and slapped their hands upon their mouths, united in a general war whoop. Then, at another signal from Rolling Thunder, they started the twisting, shuffling dance once more.

When they reached Bieleson and Simmons the second time, the sharp flint arrowheads were brought into use. Each warrior, as he passed, giving a wild screech, would brandish his knife or tomahawk in their faces an instant, then draw the sharp point of the stone across their naked bodies. The cuts, Roger observed, were not deep, penetrating the flesh only far enough to cause the blood to ooze out in great crimson gouts. By the time the last Comanche brave had passed, the suffering captives presented an awful spectacle. Their groans tore at Roger's nerves and even Jake Tulley looked a bit greenish around the lips. In the progress of the torture, Rolling Stone next called an intermission.

Some of the warriors threw themselves on the ground and lighted their pipes. Others collected in little groups. All of them laughed and shouted, pointing their fingers at the prisoners in derision, taunting them as cowards and thieves. Roger had opportunity to look around.

Horst Bieleson stood pale-faced and shaken, torrents of tears coursing down his face. An old woman had replaced Big Spotted Cat, so the young warrior could participate in the ceremony. She kept a hand clapped over Horst's mouth, all right, Roger noted, while with the other she constantly fondled his genitals and cooed to him that everything would be all right. He was a Comanche now and had to learn to live like one. Roger turned away and motioned to Tulley. They stepped apart from their hosts.

"It won't be long now," Roger bragged. "Things are going much easier than I expected. Sending your men on the raids has certainly improved our take."

"God. The things they do . . . an' . . . an' this. It turns my stomach."

"That's saying a lot, Jake," Roger told him dryly. "You know, I think that maybe we should have dealt with the Comanches before. They seem more intelligent and tractable than the Sioux."

"They stink. They never take a wash in the creek an' they go around with their cocks hanging out."

"Put steam in your engine, does it?"

"You son of a bitch!" Jake growled.

"Only making a joke, Jake. Relax. Nothing stands in

81

our way now. We can build a rich empire in the Panhandle. Then, if you like, I'll put you in charge of exterminating these vermin."

A beaming smile creased Jake's face. "That's more like it."

The short break lasted fifteen minutes. During it, the captives bore themselves quite differently. Bieleson uttered not a word, though his sobs and groans were of the sort that only the most intense pain and agony could wring from the human heart. Contrarily, despite his great size and blustering strength when behind the bar of his saloon, Ab Simmons issued forth pitiful cries and unceasing prayers. Constantly he exclaimed his horror aloud.

"Oh! God have mercy on me! Ah, Father in heaven pity me! Blessed Lord Jesus, come and put me out of pain!" His miserable wails began again at the signal to commence.

Roger and Jake stood frozen to the ground while the afternoon wore on and the torment continued for a good two hours. At last the final act of the fearful tragedy approached.

On their final round, the warriors halted and formed a half circle. Then two of them moved out from the center and struck the postures of a war dance, raising their voices in the scalp song. They advanced and receded, moving now to the right, then the left. For more than ten minutes this went on, in which they covered as many paces. Finally they reached their victims. For a short while they danced before them, then raised their steel trade hatchets and brought the sharp, shining blades crashing down through the captives' skulls. At once, the bodies were taken down and rudely thrown upon the ground. As the performers and the audience broke up, camp dogs fell on the corpses and began to devour the tenderest parts.

"Christ!" Jake Tulley gasped. "I'll never eat dog in this camp again."

"Think of it as an exercise in self-control," Roger advised him. "A month from now, we shall be rulers of all we survey."

Far off, beyond the southeastern horizon, a yellow-brown smudge of coal and wood fires marked the location of San Angelo, Texas. After leaving the train there, Lord Southington's hunting expedition, with Rebecca and Lone Wolf along, had made a long day's journey toward the Panhandle. Their vast clutter of accouterments and livestock had made the train trip from Austin without incident or damage. With twilight approaching, Issac Curleyhead and Lone Wolf had ridden ahead to locate a suitable campsite for the convoy. Rebecca cantered beside Jason Plumm, at which place Lady Priscilla found her when she rode up and insinuated herself between the young couple.

"I hope you don't mind," Lady Priscilla began, meaning the exact opposite, "but I'm curious about when we will be stopping."

"No imposition at all," Rebecca informed her, killing the woman with her eyes. "Lone Wolf will let us know where and when. Not more than another hour, you can be sure of that."

"Thank you, ever so much," Priscilla gushed insincerely. "Couldn't you just hurry along and find him for us?" Bile dripped from each word.

"If it's all the same, I'll stay here," Rebecca answered tightly. She hauled on Ike's reins and seesawed around Lady Priscilla and Jason, so that she came up on his opposite side. "Jason has been telling me the most fascinating things about England." Her thin-edged smile could have slit a certain overly long feminine throat.

A dry-gourd, whispering buzz erupted from the fetlock-high grass in front of them. Instantly the horses flinched and neighed in fright, their skins rippling with nervousness. They all saw it then. A huge, fat prairie rattler, all of six feet in length, coiled and ready to strike.

Lady Priscilla shrieked in horror.

Rebecca drew one of her replacement American .44s from the saddle holsters with surprising speed, considering her size and the revolver's weight. As it cleared leather, she cocked the hammer and let it go, firing by instinctive point aim.

The big .44 slug sprayed rattlesnake brains across the prairie and the headless monster writhed and flopped in the grass, still attempting to deliver its vanished deadly venom on a victim it could no longer see.

Priscilla continued to scream and, combined with the smell of blood, the shot, and sight of the thrashing snake, her mount took off like a rabid dog across the prairie. Lady Priscilla, confined in a sidesaddle, flopped about like a doll strapped to its back.

Rebecca urged Ike forward in a bolting gallop. Slowly she closed the distance between her and the hysterical woman. The undirected mount swung first one way then the next. It defied Rebecca's ability to outguess it and make a direct line dash to intercept.

The two horses plunged on over the turf, hoofs casting up great divots of black soil and tall, brown buffalo grass. Ahead of her, Rebecca watched as Lady Priscilla's gelding hauled her through a small stand of sage. The beast instantly changed course.

This time, Rebecca had the measure of it. She urged Ike to greater speed and closed in on the churning rump of the roan. Lady Priscilla continued to yell and flail her arms uselessly. Foolishly she had tied the reins together and they rested on the surging neck of her gelding. Rebecca reached out and tried to get a hold on one of Priscilla's hands. The noblewoman shrilled again and flung herself away.

Rebecca punished Ike's ribs and gathered a final burst of power. Neck and neck, she reached over, retrieved the loose reins and began slowing.

"Whoa, boy. Whoa, there. Easy now," she cooed to the wall-eyed horse. "That's it. Slow up. Whoa-whoa-whoa."

With a nervous snort, the panicked animal wound down to a trot, then a walk. At last, shivering and foam-flecked it halted.

"From now on, don't tie your reins," Rebecca recommended. "And it would be wise to ride a Spanish saddle. You can control the horse better and it protects you from a dangerous fall."

"What? Why, no lady would ever consent to sit astraddle of a horse. It's . . . obscene."

"I appreciate your gratitude for getting you stopped," Rebecca replied nastily.

Fuming at Rebecca's obvious superiority on the plains, her prowess in riding and quick-thinking ability to react to the situation, Lady Priscilla flung her head in a haughty gesture and curled her lips into a sneer.

"He would have stopped."

"Eventually. By then you would have very likely had your brains splattered all over Texas like that rattler. There are a million ways to die out here. Don't make it easy."

"Damn your insolence!" Lady Priscilla spat. She

started to say more, but Jason rode up, with Christopher at his side.

"You were magnificent," the young lord cried, embracing Rebecca.

Over Jason's shoulder, the white squaw saw the fires of Hell kindled in Lady Priscilla's eyes.

EIGHT

Juan Guyardo had been born in the Basque region of the Pyrenees Mountains in Spain. He grew up on a large sheep station and, when he came to the United States, naturally enough he went to work for a sheep rancher. He loved the sprawling plains of Texas where, as he often put it to his fellow shepherds, a man can see forever. He tended his flocks with care and took pride in the great quantities of wool they produced and the tender, flavorful meat. He had three dogs for working the woolly animals.

Two of them currently circled the flock, while the last lay dead at the feet of *Nis-ti-u-na*.

Wild Horse looked down at the lifeless creature as he wiped its blood from his knife on the thick fur. He rose and spoke quietly to his followers.

"Now to get the short man in the strange clothes."

To his misfortune, Juan Guyardo happened to be tending the flock nearest to the station proper. Located some twenty miles from the main ranch house, the station consisted of a large granary, to provide supplemental feed for the sheep, a long bunkhouse for use by employees and passersby, a cook shack, wash house, shearing sheds, and storage rooms for the wool. It also happened to be the next target selected by Roger Styles and Rolling Thunder.

Like an irresistible wave, the Comanche warriors and white outlaws converged on the small, house-on-wheels that Juan used as his combination bunkroom, kitchen, and storage space while on the range with his sheep. Suddenly one of the flock guards began to bark stridently.

Visions of marauding wolves flitted through Juan's mind and he awoke with a start. The dog, Pepe, he recognized by the tone of voice, continued to growl and yap. Juan crawled from his blankets, picked up his peaked knit Basque cap and a shotgun, and swung open the door of the wagon's living area.

Two shots blasted out of the pre-dawn blackness. Juan Guyardo flew backward into his rolling cottage, sprays of blood from his back staining the lacquered, rose-tinted inner walls a darker red. Juan died so that the station could be successfully raided.

The first pale pink band showed on the eastern horizon when Sagus MacDuff, the station cook, roused himself. He dressed, then crossed from the bunkhouse to the kitchen. There he built fires in the cook stoves to make coffee and put a large pot of mutton stew to boil, while he began to mix dough for biscuits. Chickens clucked nervously in their pen outside and a rooster declared it to be a new day. Sagus continued to work his thick batch, flour smeared to his elbows. From the bunkhouse he heard the hacking, liquid cough of Anselmo Valdez, one of the Basque shepherds.

"Poor man," Sagus said aloud to his pots and pans. "He be dyin' o' the wastin' disease. His wee lungs is fair full wi' watery poison."

A yapping, snarling chorus from the dogs first alerted Sagus MacDuff to danger. He doused the kerosene lamp, quickly blowing on the wick, then went to one corner of the large kitchen and retrieved a shotgun that rested against the wall.

At the door, he opened it a crack and peered out. Dark figures flitted from one deep shadow pool to the next across the station compound. Sagus studied it for only a second before he knew what was happening.

"B'God it is an Indian raid," he muttered under his breath. Well, no matter. He was in a stout stone building, with five boxes of brass shotgun shells loaded with buckshot. Quickly he closed and barred the door, then went to each window and eased together the shutters. All had firing loupes and he felt secure. Then he hastened to give the alarm.

Sagus opened one shutter and blasted a running figure off its feet with a single barrel of the Greener. "Indians!" he shouted. "Ta arrrms, laddies! It's Indians!" Sagus slammed the panel shut, secured it, and contented himself to fire through the oblong firing port.

He expended the second charge and reloaded the shotgun. He winced at the sound of hideous screams that came from the bunkhouse. His warning had come too late.

"Hot damn, we're in for it now," Toby Waters yelled to Les Cramer. The shotgun blast had startled them both.

"It's those gawdamned dogs these sheep-lovers keep," Les called back. "Cain't sneak up on the bastards to save yer soul."

From ahead they heard screams that indicated the Comanche warriors had managed to get into the bunkhouse. Toby grinned. "Bunch of them furriners catchin' hell in there, huh?"

"We got our job to do," Les reminded him. "Have to get that damned cook."

Les ran forward, doubled low. His stance made him a poor target. Even so, Sagus MacDuff managed to slap the center of his shot pattern into the top of Les' head. His skull exploded like an over-ripe melon. Shards of it splattered in Toby's face and he turned aside, gagging. Sour bile rose from his stomach and spewed on the ground.

More screams came from the bunkhouse. So far the raid had gone swiftly, despite the warning cry from the cook. By the time full light glowed in the east, only Sagus remained alive, forted up in the stone cookhouse, from where he blasted away at his attackers and kept them at bay.

Tulley's men found little in the way of valuables. The storage sheds stood empty, the spring shearing long since shipped to market. The ranch hands had little cash money. *Nis-ti-u-na's* Comanches quickly set scalping all the corpses and then organized an impromptu war dance.

Another hail storm of buckshot roared from the kitchen window. Men ducked and the Comanches gave them disdainful looks. They continued to stomp and whirl, their voices raised in a descant wail.

"We gotta get that sombitch outta there," Toby Waters commanded. He looked to where Sonney Boyle crouched. "Where's Opie?"

"How the hell should I know?" Sonney yelled back. "There ain't any li'l girls to fuck around here."

90

"Go find him, damnit. We gotta break into that cookhouse."

Sonney located Opie Dillon at the corral.

"Baaa! . . . Baaa! . . . Baaa!"

A young ewe hung over the middle rail of the horse corral, her body kept captive by backward pressure on her forelegs. Opie Dillon, his trousers around his knees, pressed against her backside, his buttocks churning. Sonney stared in disbelief at what went on before his eyes. His lips curled in disgust and he spat on the ground.

"Opie, you gotta be the most disgusting son of a bitch that ever walked this earth."

"What's the matter with you? There ain't no *female* females around," he said, grinning wickedly. "An' this is the next best thing. You can have seconds, Sonney, iffin you wants to."

"You're a goddamned animal!" Sonney exploded. "Get yer pecker outta that sheep and come on. We gotta bust into the cookhouse. Hurry, damnit."

Sagus MacDuff saw his besiegers gather for a serious try at the door. He waited until they charged, bunched together to carry a thick-butted length of Osage orange fence post as a battering ram. Then he gave them both barrels of the Greener, reloaded quickly and triggered off both again.

The lead men had fallen, three others staggered away, clasping gory wounds in their stomachs and chests. Dazed, the last pair on the ram jolted to a stop, turned and ran. Behind them, Sagus saw Comanche braves lighting firebrands and darting from their crazy war dance to set fire to the station buildings. Wouldn't be long before they got to him. He reloaded, raised his aim a little and gave them a shower of lead balls to discourage their efforts.

If he was doomed to die, he might as well do it in style, Sagus thought. He reloaded, set his shotgun aside and went to a small closet. From it he took a large cloth bag which he sat on the butcher block. He opened the drawstrings and took out a magnificent instrument. He fitted the bulbous sack under his left armpit and wet a vibrant reed with his tongue.

Then Sagus placed the chanter in his mouth and began furiously to blow up the bladder. His fingers sought the holes in a slender, belled-end tube and he gave an experimental squeeze. Silver-trimmed, beautifully carved pipes came erect and a slight wheeze emanated from the device. He puffed some more, then began to pace the room, delicately lifting fingertips from note holes as the kitchen filled with sound.

Brennan on the Moor wailed in its ghostly fashion from the bagpipe, followed by *Men of Harlech* and at last, Sagus' favorite, *Amazing Grace*.

Outside, *Nis-ti-u-na* abruptly stopped his war dance, one leg elevated in mid-stomp. What terrible monster from the dark world made such a sound?

"What the hell?" Toby Waters blurted out.

"Je-sus! What a God-awful noise!" Sonney Boyle added.

"Spirits!" Wild Horse cried. He lowered the suspended leg and began to flee toward his pony. "Spirits of the dead, come to punish us. Run, Brothers. Scatter to the winds!"

The Comanche warriors, fierce and undaunted marauders of the plains, exchanged frightened, superstitious glances and, as one man, dashed shrieking for their mounts. Left alone, the surviving members of Jake Tulley's gang had no choice but to follow them.

*   *   *

Unaware of the fiasco at the sheep station, Roger Styles sat under a canvas shade in Rolling Thunder's camp, sipping on his fine brandy and watching the daily activities. His palate longed for the flavor of pork or chicken. A pair of trout would be good, too, he thought. The Comanches never ate fowl or fish. Perhaps he would send one of Tulley's men out to bag a few prairie grouse. Roasted over mesquite wood they should be delicious. The dreary thought of another horse flesh feast, the Comanches' favorite dish, turned his stomach. His attention strayed to the figure of a comely, at least by Comanche standards, young maiden. It would be nice, he thought, his loins radiating heat, to grab her and force his attentions on her.

Then Roger recalled the scene of torture he and Tulley had been forced to witness. God, they could do that to him. His ardor cooled in the arctic blast of reality. The raiding party should be returning soon. Jake Tulley sauntered up then and Roger emptied his glass. He poured two and offered one to his partner.

"Sit down, Jake. We're winning now. There's not much left to do, you know. Only three towns stand between us and our empire. There's Ragtown in Porter County," he began to enumerate.

"You mean that place some folks are startin' to call Amarilli?"

"That's the one. Then there's Tascosa west of there in Oldham County and Sweetwater City, east of Ragtown in Wheeler County. They're more or less in a linc, so we'll organize one big sweep and get them all."

"What about this Colonel Goodnight? I hear he's already movin' cattle into Palo Duro Canyon."

"We'll deal with that son of a bitch first," Roger growled.

*   *   *

A soft breeze whispered through the tall, brown grass. Nothing else moved on the prairie except the rhythmic dip, tear, and chew of a large family of prong-horned antelope. Jason Plumm lay prone behind a large tuft and motioned silently to Rebecca that he would take the shot. Rebecca nodded agreement and watched intently as Jason eased his rifle into position against his shoulder. He took swift, expert aim and squeezed the trigger.

The big trophy buck leaped high in the air, head tossed back, mouth open in a nearly soundless wail of pain. He crashed to the ground, took two bounding steps and fell in quivering death. A split second after Jason fired, Rebecca's rifle spoke and she brought down a younger buck for the cook pot. The rest of the family thundered off across the plains.

"Good shot, Jason. Excellent, in fact."

"Thank you, Rebecca. You didn't do so badly yourself."

"Let's get them gutted and we'll start back. You'll have a beautiful trophy out of that one. I like this. Hunting with you is . . . so different than what we did in Iron Calf's camp. There it was a matter of total survival. The men hunted almost daily. In winter we nearly starved. Here . . . it's all so *free*."

Rebecca knelt by the first antelope and expertly opened it from tail to breastbone. In minutes she had both animals field dressed. Jason lifted the carcasses onto a pack mule. They washed their hands in water from Jason's canteen and swung into the saddle.

They rode back toward the route of the small convoy talking pleasantly about Jason's ambitions for this hunt. Half an hour from the trail, Jason pointed out a tall, majestic cottonwood standing on the crown of a hill.

"Doesn't that look inviting?"

"I'll say," Rebecca answered, a wicked, enticing lilt in her voice.

"Shall we, ah, ride over and investigate?"

"I was afraid you would never ask."

When they reached the small knoll, Jason drove picket pegs and secured the horses. He and Rebecca removed their clothing in a frenzied hurry and came into each other's arms. They kissed and caressed with mounting fervor, breath coming in gasps. Slowly Rebecca sank to her knees and took his engorged phallus in her hands. One hand gently cupped his throbbing scrotum and playfully squeezed. With the other, she began to stroke his long, slender manhood. He sighted contentedly, then gasped as shivers of pleasure flashed through his sensitive skin when Rebecca closed her tender lips over the fiery head of his pulsating penis.

"Aaah. Becky, Becky, so smooth. So very good. Deeper! Take it all."

With practiced skill she worked to do his bidding.

After a long, ecstatic procession upward to the pinnacle of his delight, Jason exploded into shards of fragile, multi-colored light. When the tremendous sensation subsided, he tenderly positioned Rebecca on the soft grass under the spreading boughs and came to her in an insistent thrust that popped her eyes wide open and brought a shrill of delight from deep in her chest. Slowly, deliciously, they made love through the long hours of the afternoon.

NINE

Sagus MacDuff rode through the day, exhausting one horse and exchanging it for another, spreading the word of the Comanche attack. Shortly before daylight, he again turned in a worn mount and pressed on. Behind him, a roused populace girded themselves to face the howling bands of the dread Comanches and hurriedly brought in stock and provisioned root cellars as havens for women and children. Reeling from hunger, Sagus stopped long enough at noon the second day to gulp down a meal, then raced onward. He ran two more horses into the ground before he reached his goal.

Late in the afternoon of the third day following the raid on his sheep station, Sagus, weary and barely conscious, pounded into Lubbock. He asked directions and went directly to the headquarters of the Frontier Company of the Texas Rangers. He nearly collapsed when he rushed into the orderly room.

"What's this?" a man behind the desk demanded.

"Comanches. Indian raid in Deaf Smith County. The Six-Bar-Oh Ranch."

The tough ranger behind the desk rose and caught MacDuff before he could fall. He eased the sagging man to a chair. "Sit down here a minute. I'll get the captain." He walked to a door and rapped lightly. "Cap'n. There's a man out here I think you oughtta see. Says he's ridden all the way from Deaf Smith County. Injun raids."

Captain Alan Slone came out of his private office and looked at the disheveled MacDuff. The ranger officer had rugged features, a big handlebar mustache drooped around his small mouth and shrewd wide-set brown eyes twinkled under thick, bushy brows. He wore rough clothes and rundown boots, a scarred leather belt circled his waist, from which hung a brace of holsters, filled with heavy-framed Colt's revolvers. The bone slab handles of a Bowie knife showed above the line of cartridges in loops at the back. Only the big circular badge with its bold star and the legend, "Texas Rangers" gave any indication of rank or authority.

"Better let me hear it from the start," he commanded, crossing to where Sagus sagged in the chair.

Quickly, between gulps from a clay cup of water, the Scots sheepman told his story. As he progressed, Captain Slone developed an increasing scowl. An unruly shock of his dark brown hair fell over his forehead and, so engrossed had he become, he did not brush it away in his habitual manner.

While he talked, Sagus noticed another knife tucked into the ranger captain's belt on the left side and, when Slone cocked one scuffed boot on a chair, face intent on the details of Sagus' story, the Scotsman saw a thin stiletto inserted between the lining and the outer leather.

"You are positive there were white men with the

Comanches?" Slone asked when the narrative ended. "Comancheros?"

"I . . . don't think so. They didn't look like the usual type. Nerra a scalp on their shirts or belts. None of them seemed to understand what the Comanches said, either. Like two groups fightin' together wi'out a common leader."

"And this happened when?"

"Three day ago, this mornin'."

"You were the only survivor?"

"Aye. That I am, laddie. There was no torture goin' on after the shootin' ended. Nerra a lad survived. They coom at us ta fast an' ta many. Even the wee doggies were butchered."

"How was it that you got away?"

"Why, mon . . . I dinna rightly know. Yon heathen bastards done took in a fright, though, when I began to make ready for dyin'."

"How is that?"

"Why, ken ye knicht? Wi' the pipes, mon. I took to skirlin' on me bagpipe."

Despite the seriousness of the situation and the depleted condition of his informant, Captain Slone began to howl with laughter. When he recovered he explained himself. "I can just see that now. Those ignorant, superstitious hostiles all worked up to a war dance after a little killing and then comes this awful caterwauling, like some dreadful sound out of a graveyard."

"Awful? What would be so awful about the pipes, mon? Kin ye tell me that?"

Captain Slone ignored the question. Instead he issued crisp orders to assemble the company, with a week's rations, and make ready to ride north.

*   *   *

Fox crouched low behind the brow of a hill and looked down on the surprising scene below. Two of the oddest-looking wagons he had ever encountered swayed and rumbled over the rough ground. A tempting string of pack mules strung out behind and several people on horseback rode ahead. His eyes narrowed when he recognized one of the deadly pack of turncoats who lived in the white way. Delaware they were called. He waited patiently, counting the number of his enemy carefully.

Satisfied at last, he withdrew and reclaimed his pony. A short ride brought him to the small raiding party that accompanied him. Quickly he outlined what he had seen.

"Three women. Two with the yellow hair of the whites, another who wears the doeskin dress and braided black hair of our enemy to the north, the Sioux." Fox made the cutthroat sign for the feared tribe. "Two men are of the forest people who now live on our plains. Four more men who wear strange clothes and stare at the land like lost souls. There is another who looks like them, yet he rides a horse well and shows no fear. The last bothers me. He sits his pony like an *Absaroka*, tracks like one and talks with the Delaware like a brother. He could be dangerous. There is also a small boy."

"Then we will attack them?" an anxious young brave asked.

"We will see. First, you will ride to *Kansaleumko* and tell him what we have seen. The rest will follow the trail and learn what we can. When the sun is overhead two sleeps from now, we will know what our war chief wishes done."

*   *   *

Jason Plumm's entourage halted for the night some three hours later. When the camp had been set up, Jason came to Rebecca and Lone Wolf.

"I know you are somewhat in a hurry to get to the Panhandle, but I really would like to spend a couple of days here. It looks to be prime hunting country."

"Yes," Rebecca agreed. "I saw signs of buffalo. There might be a large herd nearby."

"Ah! Bison." Jason's eyes lighted with expectation. "That is what I am most interested in bagging. I hear they are rather good to eat."

Lone Wolf smiled. "There's nothing sweeter than roasted hump meat. Or juicy back ribs, right out from under the hump. Best eatin' in the world. You can do what you want with the head and hide, but we will definitely have to feast on the rest."

"Your enthusiasm reassures me," Jason said through a smile.

Christopher came up, a long white towel and cake of yellow lye soap in one hand. "Uncle Jason, Basil is taking me to the stream for a bathe. I shan't be long."

"Run along, then, Chris." Jason dismissed the boy.

Lone Wolf had been surreptitiously studying the flighty wine steward since the beginning of the trip. The man knew his wines and spoke rapturously of them and he waxed enthusiastic over exotic foods. Other than that, Lone Wolf had little use for him. Basil winced every time a rifle went off and cringed from cleaning game. For that reason, Lone Wolf's remark held more seriousness than jest.

"I'd keep an eye on Sweet Basil, were I you, Chris."

Astute and worldly wise from experiences in his boarding school, Chris answered him levelly, their eyes locked in mutual understanding, though his face reflected only boyish innocence. "Oh, Basil and I have

101

an understanding. He keeps his hands off me and I don't *accidentally* shoot out his bloody brains. Ta."

The youngster trotted off with eagerness to wash away the day's accumulated soreness and be afforded the luxury of an hour's play in the water.

Once the evening meal had been put behind and night had settled like a black velvet cloak over the prairie, Jason and Rebecca wandered away to the creek bank under a Tiffany display of celestial diamonds. An Indian summer held the land in warmth, and soft scents of sage, woodsmoke, and prairie flowers made the evening heady with their lush aromas.

Jason had brought along a blanket and spread it under the overhanging branches of a willow. Screened from their surroundings, their hands soon began to avidly explore each other's body. Jason's strong fingers soon brought stiff life to the thick buds of Rebecca's nipples. She, in turn, unbuttoned his shirt and laid her hand against his chest. Her tongue licked at him like a salt-starved deer.

Gently he lifted the hem of her doeskin dress and stroked the satin delight of her thighs. Heat radiated from above and he sought its source. His thumb entered the cleft in her nearly hairless mound and parted the moist, lacy folds as he progressed upward. Diligently he rubbed against the growing protrusion at the top while Rebecca sighed her contentment. He felt her fingers at the buttons of his trousers and a moment later, their welcome coolness as they encircled his rigid organ. Slowly she began to stroke him.

"Hurry," she urged him. "Let's get undressed."

The word being as good as the deed, they soon had their garments in a welter to one side while their naked flesh clung together in mounting passion. Jason's vibrating rapier pressed into the hollow of her stomach and sought to make a new place of entry. Her arms encircled him and their lips met.

Rebecca's tongue probed deeply within his mouth, searching, teasing, inviting him to greater accomplishments. She began to moan softly as he once more started to manipulate her tender, responsive gateway.

"Now," she begged. "Take me now, darling. I . . . can't . . . stand . . . it!"

Jason adjusted himself and, with her guidance, swiftly and deeply penetrated to the core of her being. She rose to meet him with a ferocity that rivaled his own consuming need. Then, with languid motions they rocked the minutes away, clasped in shared pleasure, beyond reach by the conscious world.

In their second flight to the stars, Rebecca peaked twice and patiently drew Jason toward his mighty explosion. By careful control of her skillful muscles, which sent tremblers of delight through her, she built tension in them both as they approached the moment and prolonged it until they blazed into infinity together. The same powerful rings gripped at his spasming shaft and drew the final drop of nectar from its turgid tip. At last, reluctantly, they parted.

They reclined, sated for the moment, only to be jerked upright by a stifled gasp from beyond the willow branches.

"Christopher! What the bloody hell are you doing there?" Jason demanded in a harsh whisper.

"Oh, sweet heavens," the boy stammered. "I . . . I've made a sticky mess of things, I have." Then he seemed to recover himself and replied to his uncle's query. "N-nothing, Uncle Jason. Honestly. I . . . only went for a walk."

"Step closer. Now, I want an explanation, young man."

"Yes, sir. You see, I am quite a bit sore from all the horseback riding of late. Wouldn't let me get to sleep.

So I thought, a bit of a stroll, wet my feet in the stream, that sort of thing. I didn't know you were here."

"Come forward," Jason commanded. The lad obeyed, standing before them with his hands crossed over his groin. "How much did you see?"

Christopher dropped his gaze to the ground. "Too much, I'm afraid."

"I'm sure you don't understand exactly what you . . . that is to say, adults often engage in certain, ah, experiences that are not fully perceived by children," Jason ended lamely.

Beside him, Rebecca sat huddled in on herself, her doeskin dress held upward like a shield.

In the dim light, Christopher's face darkened with embarrassment. "Oh, I won't tell, Uncle Jason. That's a promise."

"I'm sure you won't, son. It's only . . . only, do you know what I mean?"

A fleeting smile touched the boy's lips. "I . . . think so. That's something grownups do and not a matter that I should be stumbling on in the dark."

"Quite right. Now, run along. And seal those lips, what?"

"Oh, yes." Christopher's face flamed as he hurried along the creek bank. Heat likewise radiated from his loins where that rebellious protrusion remained disturbingly rigid, though his discovery and subsequent interrogation should have withered it away long ago.

Behind him, Jason moved to comfort Rebecca who sat with head bowed, shoulders shaking. "There, there, now. It will be all right."

"Oh, Jason, Jason. It's not that. I . . . I don't know whether to laugh or cry."

TEN

"Uncle Jason! Uncle Jason!" Christopher yelled as he ran through the pre-dawn stillness of the camp. "Someone stole my horse. And there are three mules missing, too."

Everyone came instantly awake in the small encampment. Lone Wolf exchanged a significant glance with the two Delaware and they set out to scour the area. Rebecca did likewise, taking the direction the others had left uncovered.

"They came in from the downwind side," Rebecca announced a few minutes later. She pointed to slight traces of small moccasin prints on the ground outside camp.

"They?" Sir Devon Windemire huffed. "Good Lord, do you mean some large number of people invaded our campsite during the night?"

"Only four of them," Rebecca returned.

"Definitely Indians," Lone Wolf added as he came from where he had been examining the area around the picket line.

Issac Curleyhead bent low over the sign and rose with a frown. When his partner trotted over, they again studied the marks and held a short conversation in their own language. At last Cootyarkey Journeycake pointed to the west and spoke a single word to Issac.

"Woondhunaayoongk."

Issac nodded and stroked a small, sickle-shaped scar on his chin. He turned to the waiting whites. "From what Coot saw, they went to the west. Come in this way, circle around, cut off three mules and the horse, then go out that way. Comanche."

"Yes," Journeycake agreed. "Comanche."

"We'll all be killed!" Lady Priscilla shrieked.

"Get ahold of yourself, my dear," Anthony Parrish told his wife. "If they walked around our camp like that in the night, they could have as easily slit all our throats."

"This was not a war party," Rebecca informed them.

"Even so, why weren't we attacked?" Sir Devon demanded.

"From the size of the moccasin prints," Rebecca went on, "it must have been some boys. Youngsters are taken along on hunting and war parties to do camp work, tend the horses, skin game. Often these boys work themselves up into a pitch and, when there is an opportunity, go out on a horse-stealing expedition all on their own. It's not approved of by their elders, but they are rarely punished for it. Particularly if they carry it off without any injuries or deaths."

"How barbaric," the portly Sir Devon declared. "I say, could this sort of thing go on all the while we're here?"

"Not likely. Hunting parties move around a lot. Given the direction they went off with our stock, the whole party is probably moving south and west.

Provided we keep watch, we should be safe from now on," Lone Wolf remarked.

Cootyarkey shook his long head in solemn disagreement. "Comanches are *always* looking for a fight. They hate whites and it is my guess they will punish these boys for letting us know that there are Comanches around. We had better move camp. Issac and I will ride a wide scout around our line of travel. Lone Wolf, you know what to do."

"What about me?" Rebecca demanded, her pride again stung by heavy-handed male superiority.

"Somone has to take care of our babes in the woods," Issac told her in fractured Lakota. He added a smile that included her in the conspiracy to minimize the danger for the English party's benefit.

"Yes," she answered back. "Of course. Jason and I can look around on our own and perhaps spot some buffalo. One thing, though," she added. "Everyone should have a weapon close at hand."

"That's it, then," Jason said brightly. "We'll have a quick breakfast and push on."

"I say, Jason," Sir Devon began as he walked away with the young lord. "This running around with loaded arms and the like. Sounds confounded dangerous to me. I think there's something they're not telling us. Why, we could be attacked by these bloody savages at any moment."

"Don't worry, Dev. We're in good hands. Besides, with the long-range double-bore rifles we brought with us, we can handle anything that comes along."

Once loaded, the caravan covered ten rapid miles, the spindly wheels of the hearselike wagons threatening to splinter on each rock and rut. Far in the lead, alert

107

for any signs of hostile Comanches, Lone Wolf subtly changed the route to more nearly due north. It would, he felt, take them away from the probable course followed by the Indians. Rebecca and Jason rode at a tangent to the wagons, ahead and angled eastward. About noon, she reined up abruptly and extended her arm, pointing a finger at what appeared to be a cluster of low, brownish-black mounds, obscured by a faint haze on the horizon.

"There they are," she told her companion.

"What? The savages?"

"Buffalo. A small herd. Probably not more than three hundred. We can cut due west from here and intercept the wagons. I'll send Christopher forward with word to Lone Wolf. We can set up camp and you will get your buffalo."

Jason smiled at her. "What are we waiting for?"

True to her estimation, Rebecca and Jason caught sight of the wagons after only a half-hour ride to the west. Swelled with pride in the importance of his errand, Christopher quickly saddled a spare mount and made ready to ride off to find Lone Wolf. Rebecca gave him a final instruction.

"Look along the way for any small pile of stones or buffalo chips. Whichever side of the trail they are on indicates a turn in the direction. Keep your eyes open, follow those and you'll have no trouble locating Lone Wolf."

"Right-o, Miss Rebecca. I'm off then." With a wild yell of youthful exuberance, Christopher raced away.

"Aren't you being rather inconsiderate of his safety?" Lady Priscilla asked icily. "After all, he is only a small boy and there is the danger of these aborigines falling upon us."

"Every child has to grow up sometime," Rebecca answered her levelly. "By the age of eight, any Oglala boy could do what Chris is attempting."

"B-but, those are primitives you're talking about. Savages."

"Aren't all children?" Rebecca countered sweetly, mocking one of Lady Priscilla's favorite complaints.

At her direction, with Jason riding beside her, Rebecca led the small convoy to the east in pursuit of the buffalo herd. They encountered Cootyarkey a few minutes later, on one of his back and forth sweeps, and he set out to notify Issac, who patrolled the other flank. Slowly the wagons rolled on. Rebecca rode forward with Jason and located a spot near enough to keep the herd in sight, yet far enough away to keep from spooking the animals.

"We'll make camp when they catch up. There will be light enough to get in a hunt and we can have buffalo hump and a smoked tongue for supper tonight."

"Marvelous. As you are, my dear." Jason reached out to stroke Rebecca's glistening black braids. She moved slightly away from him.

"There are times, Jason, when . . ."

"What is it? Have I done something wrong?"

"Not wrong, so much as . . . unthinking. When you are around the other men, you, ah, seem to tuck me off in a corner, expect me to be content with the company of the other women. My opinion isn't consulted on matters such as the Comanches, or the trail we'll take."

"But you *are* a woman," he protested. "Of course you should be catered to and sheltered, like women expect to be treated. Isn't it enough that I think I'm falling in love with you? I don't want an *equal*, I want a woman I can idolize and protect. That's . . . that's what love is all about, isn't it?"

"I . . . I'm not certain. I've had that sort of rela-tionship. Yet . . ." Rebecca sighed and tried a new approach. "You don't know a great deal about me, Jason."

"That's true. I've sort of expected you would, in your own way and in good time, tell me more. Frankly, I'm curious. Why have you come to Texas? We have certainly heard news enough about Indian uprisings. It's risky enough for a well-armed party like ours. Yet you and Lone Wolf had every intention of coming way out here, just the two of you."

"I told you I had been a captive of the Oglala. And that I am half Sioux myself. That isn't all of it, Jason. You see, I was traded off to Iron Calf and his Oglala band by a man named Jake Tulley and my two uncles, Ezekiel and Virgil Caldwell."

"Why . . . that's outrageous!"

"Let me finish." Quickly she told Jason the highlights of her captivity, her marriage to Four Horns, the child they had, and of their deaths. She also mentioned her second marriage, which had amounted to little more than slavery. Jason listened fascinated and did not interrupt. Then, with the wagons in sight on the distant horizon, she started in on her search for vengeance. Jason's features formed a grim visage by the time she summed up her past.

"Not long ago, in New Orleans, I told a very nice young man that I had killed more than fifteen men in search of revenge. It's true. I had long ago quit counting. I have no idea how many I've sent off to the Great Spirit . . . or the pits of Hell, depending on how you look at it.

"Now, I am convinced that Bitter Creek Jake and his gang are behind these uprisings in the Panhandle. Lone Wolf and I are here to find Tulley, so I can look him in the eye while I kill him."

"My . . . word. I . . . first of all, I want you to know that what you've told me makes no difference in how I feel toward you. If anything," he emitted a nervous chuckle, "it makes me see you in a clearer, and more desirable light. As to your earlier complaint about the manner in which you are excluded from making decisions, I'm not certain this will change things. I still want to cosset you and pamper you like a man does any lovely woman. Even so, I'll not attempt to dissuade you from your purpose. I gather that is a mistake your young man in New Orleans made."

"It is," Rebecca answered a bit coldly. "But, Jason, please try to understand. I have made the decisions that count in my life since my first husband died. I chose to live with another man until circumstances permitted me to escape from the Oglala. Since then, I called the tune. I directed our efforts against Tulley. The successes were mine and so were the failures. I must see this through and I can't do that if I 'keep my place' like a proper woman should. When we reach the point where we leave your group to go after Tulley, I'll probably never see you again."

"No. Don't say that. It's something I can't bear to hear."

Then they were in each other's arms, kissing, much to the discomfiture of their horses.

"There are two ways to hunt buffalo," Rebecca lectured the British hunters an hour later. "The Indian way, which is to ride down on the beasts and kill them with arrow or lance, or shoot them through the heart. White men try to maintain what they call a stand. They set up at extreme long range and pick their targets carefully. Buffalo are slow-witted. So long as the dead are not piling up two or more in a spot, they remain unaware that anything is wrong. Only when their numbers thin down and the survivors are surrounded

111

by corpses do they become restless. By then it is too late.

"We're not here to kill that many. We could not eat the meat and it would be wasteful to slaughter animals for no reason. We'll pick a yearling calf or two for meat, take the best heads for your trophy collection, and let the rest go. Is that clear?"

Sir Devon muttered behind his mustache and placed long, interlaced fingers on his protruding belly. He was clearly ill at ease being lectured to by a woman. "I say, isn't there a theory currently popular in this country that if all the bison are killed off, the savages will either die out or come in to the preserves provided for them and become domesticated?"

A hard light of anger flared momentarily in Rebecca's eyes. "Yes," she acknowledged icily. "That idea has been put forward by some military figures. One of them answered for it not long ago at a place called the Little Big Horn."

"What I mean is, wouldn't we be doing some sort of service for your government if we were to eliminate this entire herd?"

"Sir Devon, are you a sportsman or a butcher? Why waste all that good food? We might want to eat one later. Or someone else may. From what Coot Journeycake tells me, the buffalo are almost entirely extinct in Texas already. Without them, the Comanche and other tribes raid white ranches for cattle to eat. People die as a result. We'd be doing no one a favor."

"But surely the natives could be put onto these preserves?"

"Not unless they want to go . . . or are forced to at bayonet point."

"Oh-ho! Jolly good that. Show them a little cold steel."

"Try that on the next Comanche who slips into our

112

camp," Rebecca snapped. She quickly reined in her temper. What was she doing siding with hostile Indians after all she'd been through? She drew a deep breath and tried to make amends.

"I'm sorry, Sir Devon. I'm sure you all know I spent five years as a captive in an Oglala camp. Sometimes I forget exactly who I am. I was hasty in what I said."

Sir Devon tut-tutted a bit. "Quite all right, dear girl. No offense taken. Shall we, ah, get to it?"

"I don't see why not," Rebecca answered with relief. "Pick your spots and do so with care. Two to three hundred yards would be best. Then don't shoot unless you have a sure kill." Rebecca turned to Lady Priscilla, the last flames of her momentary anger heating her words. "A woman's proper place on a buffalo hunt, at least among the Indians, is to skin the kills, dress them out and butcher the meat and flense the hides. Would you like to learn?"

"Certainly not," Lady Priscilla snapped back, each word coated in acid. "I will take a position and shoot with the man."

"You might regret that," Rebecca warned, but refrained from giving details.

Following her instructions, the hunting party took twenty minutes to work themselves into position. During that time, Lone Wolf and Christopher rode into camp and tied their mounts to the picket line. They stood, quietly observing the stalk, the tall, blond white warrior explaining details to the entranced, wide-eyed boy.

Everything went well to begin with. Jason dropped a big bull first. Then Sir Devon and Lord Anthony fired nearly as one.

The herd guards jumped sideways and snorted, heads up, weak eyes sweeping the terrain, noses twitching as they sniffed the air for some indication of what caused the noise. The other creatures stopped grazing and milled about restlessly. A small calf bellowed for its mother. After a moment, the sentries quieted and the herd resumed its foraging.

For the first time, Riggs had joined the shooters. He took aim on a small bull and dropped it with a clean shot. Rebecca started his way to offer congratulations when Lady Priscilla felled a cow standing beside the yearling Riggs had shot and, unfortunately, Sir Devon downed a bull immediately behind.

In an instant, the herd exploded. At first the frightened animals ran in all directions. Then, with a sort of swirl, they settled on a course and bore down on the hunting party, all of whom were trapped afoot, far from their mounts.

Effie shrieked in horror from the seat of a distant wagon and Basil ran about the camp shouting, "Oh, my! Oh, my. Whatever shall we do?"

"Uncle Jason! Look out!" Christopher cried from the picket line. He grabbed up his short-barreled rifle and swung into the saddle of Jason Plumm's big-chested Arab. Before Rebecca could shout a warning, Christopher shot out on a line across the front of the stampeding buffalo.

ELEVEN

Lying prone in the grass, the shooters could hear nothing from their positions above the sudden, thunderous roar of a thousand hoofs pounding the hard prairie ground. Lady Priscilla Parrish looked up from loading her Purdy double-rifle and saw the undulating forms of the crazed buffalo racing down on her from barely two hundred yards away. She screamed, threw aside her weapon and attempted to run ahead of the avalanche of tons of flesh.

As she ran, she saw at her sides Jason Plumm and Sir Devon Windemire sprinting away at oblique angles. Try as she might, she could not break her stride and change course. A niggling scrap of common sense told her that her present action was suicidal yet her terror would not let her alter direction. Ahead to her left, she saw Riggs, his heavy Purdy in one hand. The valet stopped abruptly, wheeled, and raised the double-gun to his shoulder. Cooly he shot two of the herd leaders, then spun and dashed on. Pain shot through Priscilla's leg when she twisted her ankle in a squirrel hole. Her pace slacked as she limped onward.

Rebecca had already swung into Ike's saddle at the sight of Christopher's hopeless attempt to rescue Jason. She charged after the youngster, only to see Lady Priscilla stumble and then limp on, her face chalky with fear. A quick glance showed the white squaw that the woman had no chance to escape a horribly messy death under the driving hoofs of the buffalo. She altered direction, swinging across the face of the stampeding animals. Rebecca bent low along the heaving side of her trusty Morgan stallion and extended an arm.

It seemed the distance closed in slow motion. The buffalo had covered another hundred yards while she had ridden only some fifty. There wouldn't be time. Then Lone Wolf flashed past her and leaned far over.

"Priss!" he shouted with all his might. "Priss! Here . . . grab ahold of me."

Blank-faced, the panicked woman turned her head in his direction, her movements a dreamy slowness that robbed the rescue attempt of more precious seconds. With an extra lurch, Lone Wolf strained outward and swung an arm around her waist. He used his mount's strength to jerk her off her feet. In a flash, he swung wide and streaked off away from the charging beasts.

Lady Priscilla's control snapped and she shrieked in horrified frenzy as the herd drew nearer, despite the valiant efforts of the Kiowa pony to widen the gap.

At Lone Wolf's appearance, Rebecca swerved off and headed toward Sir Devon and Anthony Parrish. "This way," she called.

They responded with alacrity, legs churning as they ran away from the edge of the advancing doom.

116

Rebecca led the way to a slight rise. The men dropped to the ground, gasping and shaken. A quick glance ahead of the stampede showed Rebecca that Jason had outdistanced the leaders and swung away to the side. Only Christopher remained unaccounted for. Then she saw him.

The small boy clung to the saddle and fought his rearing, frightened mount. His face had gone stark white and he gripped the saddle horn with all his strength. Less than a hundred yards separated him from destruction under crushing tons of blindly charging buffalo. Rebecca leaped her horse forward, unmindful of personal danger. Her heels drummed a rapid tattoo against Ike's straining sides and she shouted over and over in her mind, Hurry! Hurry!

Little by little she gained on the helpless boy. All the while the buffalo bore down on them with inexorable speed. At last she reached Christopher's side.

"Chris! Jump free," she yelled over the tumult as she swung an arm around his slender chest.

Christopher came free of the stirrups and into Rebecca's arms. His horse streaked away to his own safety as the tightly clinging pair raced off in the other direction on Ike's sweat-streaked, powerful back. The big Morgan stallion stumbled and nearly fell when the wide side of a mountain-sized buffalo on the flank of the stampede brushed his rump. Another second and Rebecca had brought Christopher to safety.

"I . . . I don't know the words to thank you," Christopher gasped out after the booming roar of the racing herd faded away. He had not taken his arms from around Rebecca's neck and now he drew himself up until their lips touched. His kiss was long and warm. When he drew back, a glowing light of pure love illuminated his eyes.

117

"You saved m-my life," he stammered. "I'll never forget you."

Fox finished the final touches with the black paint and handed the pot to a warrior nearby. Then he reached for the white. The four boys who had stolen the livestock from the whites the previous night stood before him, heads hung. Their hair had been shorn, except for a fluffy roach that extended down to the nape of their necks. Their faces and bald pates had been painted black.

Now Fox smeared white bands the length of the tufts of hair left them. They would wear their shame visibly before all the band until they redeemed themselves with some act of valor or cunning.

"Skunk cubs," Fox told them. "So you shall be until you erase the shame you bring on this war party by your foolish acts. We ride now to *Kansaleumko's* camp."

They arrived in the middle of the next day. Excitement rose, along with derisive jeers for the impetuous youngsters who had robbed Fox of surprise over the enemy. More cheering greeted the words Fox spoke regarding the strange caravan. When he finished explaining, Roger Styles approached and asked to speak with him for a while.

Roger took Fox to his shaded pavilion and poured brandy for both. "Now, tell me. What did these people look like. You described them as two different sorts."

Fox studied the matter a moment. "One wore the beaded doeskin dress of the Sioux women. She is young, beautiful. Make good to warm sleeping robes. Long black braids. Skin not dark. Other is a white man who rides, walks, like the Crow." He continued his description while an unholy light began to glow in Roger's eyes. When Fox finished, Roger sent for Jake Tulley.

"I think your old nemesis, Rebecca Caldwell, is within a day's ride of here."

"What! By all that's holy, that can only mean trouble."

"Not so hasty, Jake. Think a moment. We have nearly a hundred warriors in this encampment, and fifteen of your men. Why not ride over and pay a little call on Miss Caldwell? One she will never recover from?"

Jake burst into a gleeful smile. "Yeah. Me'n the boys could tear up a bunch like Fox described. We'll take Fox and some o' his braves along. It'll look like just another renegade killin'."

"Now you're thinking, Jake. Let's talk to Fox."

Within half an hour, Fox rode through the camp, holding high a pipe and calling for men to smoke with him and take the war path. Great excitement reigned. Twenty men agreed to take up the pipe. Tulley selected ten of his men and they hastily prepared for the expedition. Two scouts rode suddenly into the gathering, shouting their news in high, singsong voices.

"The rangers come. Texas Rangers," they cried. "Many hands of the white-eyes warriors ride our way from the south. They look for fight. We give 'em big fight, you bet you!"

TWELVE

By evening, the horrors of the stampede had diminished somewhat. Monson prepared buffalo hump under Rebecca's directions and the result came out as though the master chef had been cooking the delicacy all his life. Basil, still a bit shaken by events, produced an excellent claret to wash down the juicy slabs of alternating fat and flesh. One of the clever folding tables remained out after the meal. Jason put a kerosene lamp on it and a large, squarish wooden box.

He opened the lid and removed a variety of tools, including a decapper, case-trimming reamer, a case-length gauge and a straight line bullet seater. Seated before the array, he began to reload expended cartridges.

After a careful examination, the paper-patched .450 bullets were set to one side. With a powder measure he filled the recapped and sized brass casings and then placed a slug in the open end of a cartridge, driving it home with the bullet seater. Rebecca recalled many similar scenes in Iron Calf's camp. Powder and lead were to be had in quantity, even by the Sioux. Factory loaded ammunition was rarely to be easily found. Reloading became a matter of survival. It was slow, demanding work, she considered. While Monson, Basil, and Effie cared for the elaborate Spode china dishware on which the meal had been served, Rebecca sauntered to the table, took a second chair and sat to talk with Jason.

As he pressed the lever to seat another bullet, Lady Priscilla walked through camp, headed out in the direction taken earlier by Lone Wolf. She found him crouched in a blanket behind a clump of sage, peering out into the night.

"Is there . . . really any danger?" she asked as she settled herself on the ground at Lone Wolf's side.

"Not necessarily. It is wise to keep a watch, though. Coot and Issac will be spelling me during the night."

"What if someone were to come from another direction?"

"I can see well enough from here. With only two moves, I can cover the entire perimeter once each hour. All of the places I've selected overlap on the field of view."

"That's very clever," Lady Priscilla enthused. She placed a hand lightly on Lone Wolf's chest. "I want to thank you again for saving my life this afternoon. I was certain I would die in the next instant. Then . . . there you came. I . . . I want to offer you a rather special sort of thanks."

Despite his vow, Lone Wolf felt a stirring in his loins. He had no doubt of the attractive noblewoman's meaning. She offered herself. He recited in his mind a Crow medicine prayer to quell the desire that rose in his healthy young body. Denying himself any sexual release was the path to spiritual power, a wise old shaman had told him. The price he paid sometimes seemed inordinately high. Lady Priscilla moved closer.

"I don't wish to appear brazen, or even forward. It's only that . . . well, there is no other way of putting it. I feel such gratitude and relief. It's like I'm alive for the first time, having come so close to death. And . . ." She leaned forward until her lips touched his.

It was a cool, almost impersonal kiss. One, she realized with a start, that Lone Wolf did not return. She drew away.

"Don't I . . . please you?"

"It's not that. You see, I have taken a vow to follow the Power Road to seek the Great Spirit. In order to keep my high-self pure, I have taken an oath to remain celibate."

His answer shocked her. Worse, she didn't believe him. "You . . . you're not a pagan savage. You are as white as I am. You have a Christian name. Why do you follow these superstitions?"

"It is not superstition. It works. Believe me. I . . . I'm sorry that my situation bothers you so much. I . . ."

"Bothers me! I . . . I come out here and offer my soul to you in gratitude and you give me some story about a vow to the . . . the Great Spirit. Ach! I think I deserve better than that. It's that black-haired vixen, isn't it? You're her lover, aren't you?"

"Rebecca and I are companions. Friends, I like to think. There's nothing else between us."

"I don't believe you."

"I'm sorry. You're an attractive woman and I don't wish to distress you."

Lady Priscilla rose abruptly, her heavy skirt rustling in the still night. Her hands trembled from the rage and hurt that built within her. "Oh, don't be sorry on my account," she snapped bitterly. "I . . . I don't know what came over me." She turned on one heel and strode stiffly away, head erect on her long neck, back held rigidly.

When she reached the campsite, the first person she saw was Rebecca, sitting close at Jason's side while he loaded his ammunition. The dark-haired girl looked up with her startling blue eyes, and with an effort spoke pleasantly.

"Have a nice stroll?"

Lady Priscilla walked directly to her and swung her right arm with all her strength. The slap sounded loud under the vault of the prairie sky, and it left a red palm mark on Rebecca's cheek.

"You slut!" she screeched at Rebecca.

What happened next would have never been considered by the British peer. Rebecca sprang from her chair with the supple grace of a mountain lion. Her small hand balled into a fist, and she punched Priscilla solidly on the jaw. The noblewoman's eyes rolled up and she released a snort of breath before she wavered and fell backward.

Sprawled on the ground, she shook her head once to clear it and leaped to her feet, clawed fingers aimed for Rebecca's eyes. Rebecca side-stepped her and grabbed Priscilla's long blonde hair. She gave a mighty heave and, as Priscilla tottered backward, drove another fist to the woman's jaw.

"Priss! Rebecca! Stop that," Jason shouted. He stood so rapidly that a cartridge case fell over, spilling fine grains of black powder onto the table.

Riggs appeared, face twisted into a puzzled expression. He quickly sized up the situation and moved to come up behind Rebecca. Jason stepped toward Priscilla.

"I'll fix that pretty face of yours," Priscilla raved. "Think you can have them both, do you?" She aimed a kick for Rebecca's groin that the white squaw turned

124

easily on the outside of her left thigh.

"What the bloody hell are you talking about?" Jason demanded of them both.

Priscilla leaped forward, to catch a punch in the chest that sat her spraddle-legged in the dirt. Her husband appeared at her right. He wrung his hands, then removed his monocle and wiped it industriously.

Riggs grabbed Rebecca from behind, wrapping both arms around her so that she struggled in his grasp. At the same time Jason stepped in front of Priscilla.

"That's enough," he rasped. "Both of you. What is this all about? You're acting the bloody fool, Priscilla."

"I don't like being slapped," Rebecca announced calmly, her eyes ablaze with fighting lust.

Lady Priscilla resorted to tears. Blubbering and making no reply to Jason's question, she allowed her husband to lead her away to the wagon they used for sleeping quarters.

"I . . . I don't know what to say," Jason began by way of apology to Rebecca.

"I'm afraid I am partly at fault," Lone Wolf informed them as he strode into the firelight.

"How do you mean?" Jason asked.

"The lady sought to express her gratitude for her rescue this afternoon. I didn't respond in the manner she expected."

"Whatever are you talking about, old boy?" Sir Devon demanded as he stepped back into the firelight.

"I would rather not go into details. It's a matter between Lady Priscilla and myself." At Sir Devon's scowl, he went on. "I'm only trying, for her sake, to be discreet."

Rolling Thunder sat astride his favorite war pony at

mid-morning the next day. Hidden in the dark shadows of a narrow defile, he remained invisible to his enemy as he watched a column of Texas Rangers approach at a spirited trot. A smile creased his seamed, battle-scarred face. How easily they rode into the trap! It would be a good day for killing.

His keen eyes remained on the rangers until they passed a large split boulder. Then Rolling Thunder threw back his head and opened his mouth. A loud, ululating wolf's howl came from deep in his throat. Instantly, warriors seemed to appear from nowhere. With tufts of grass in their hair and on the backs of their hunting shirts, they rose from the ground behind and on the flanks of the rangers. Before any of the riders could react, arrows whirred through the air. Two shots sounded from the braves and a ranger toppled from his mount.

"Close up, men!" Captain Slone yelled back over the column. They would have to make a dash for it. Then he saw more Comanches, on horseback, come from the dark defile to his right front.

"Halt!" the captain bawled. "They have us surrounded. Dismount and take what cover you can. Hold your fire for my command."

Arrows flew by overhead, mingled with the crack of bullets. Captain Slone ducked low and studied the situation. The mounted Comanches appeared to be ready to launch an attack.

"Take aim to the front," he commanded. "Steady . . . hold it . . . hold it . . ."

With fierce shouts, the Comanches charged. The feather fringes on war lances rippled in the air and the warriors in the lead loosed a shower of arrows. Rapidly they closed the distance to fifty yards.

"Fire!" Captain Slone yelled. "Aim for the horses."

A rippling volley broke out and three ponies went down, heaving their riders over their heads. "Again!" the ranger officer commanded.

Rifles cracked and the aimed shots began to put new gaps in the charging line of Comanches. Suddenly a man pitched forward and lay in a spreading pool of his blood.

"They're hittin' us from behind!" a ranger shouted.

Fox watched Rolling Thunder and twenty braves charge down toward the rangers. He nodded his head knowingly and made ready. First one, then a second volley blasted from the white men who all faced toward the mounted attackers. Fox lifted his brass tack-decorated rifle stock to his shoulder and took aim. Gently he squeezed the trigger.

At once the warriors with him moved forward. As Fox stepped beyond the haze of powder smoke he saw that his aim had been true. One of the rangers lay face first in the dirt.

"Come with me!" he shouted to the others. "Take scalps! Spill blood! There are plenty *coups* for everyone."

Less than seventy yards separated the attacking Comanches when suddenly half the number of rangers faced about and fired at them. Fox heard the familiar smack of a slug hitting flesh close by his side.

"Every other man, turn about and fire," Captain Slone commanded.

Ranger Harold Prine followed the order and found another horde of Comanches, these on foot, running toward them. "Look at them heathen bastards," he called to the man closest to him.

"Makes ya think o' the Custer mess," the other ranger observed with grim humor.

Prine put his Winchester to his shoulder and fired at the first buckskin-shirted chest that filled his sights. The target stumbled backward a pace, then fell. Prine worked the lever and sought another Comanche. He fired quickly and chambered another round. Before he could take aim, an arrow thudded into the ground in front of his face. He rolled to the side and discharged another round.

A miss.

He rolled again and came face to face with a Comanche who had been crawling through the high grass toward the ring of defenders. The warrior took a startled swing with his tomahawk, and Harold Prine felt the wind of its passage over his head. No time to aim, the ranger thought. He swung his Winchester laterally and struck his adversary in the face with the narrow edge of the butt-stock.

Bone cracked and the brave uttered a bubbling scream as blood filled his mouth. A pistol discharged directly over Prine's head and he glanced up.

"Thanks, Cap'n," he told Slone.

"Keep fighting," the captain advised, then turned away to fire at another mounted Comanche.

The next second, a Comanche leaped over Prine's prone figure. The ranger rolled onto his back and swung his rifle into line. The .44-40 slug blasted out the warrior's right kidney.

*　　*　　*

Rolling Thunder scowled as he watched the progress of the battle. His confidence began to slip. He had lost too many braves for such a small force of the enemy. This should have been a swift victory. A well laid ambush and the rangers falling down in heaps, as the medicine man had predicted. Instead, they were holding their own. Something would have to be done quickly or the fight could be lost.

He raised his arm above and waved his war lance. Immediately seven white men charged out of hiding in a small ravine.

Sonney Boyle saw Rolling Thunder's signal and Jake Tulley's confirming nod. "Let's ride 'em down, boys!" he yelled at the six men with him. With an ear-shattering rebel yell, the young outlaw jumped his horse up out of the ravine, the others behind him.

They raced toward the left flank of the ranger position, six-guns blazing, their throats raw from their wild battle cries. A ranger raised up to get better aim and Sonney drew a bead on him.

The big Colt bucked in Sonney's hand and he saw the man go down. Then the man in charge shouted an order and half of the guns inside the ring swung in Sonney's direction. Smoke jetted from the leveled barrels. Quickly Sonney signaled and swung away, drawing out of range to organize another attack.

Those were white men, Captain Slone thought to himself. Right like MacDuff said. The ranger captain took careful aim and knocked the trailing man out of his saddle. "Goddamned renegades," he snarled aloud. "Pour it on, men."

The attacking force withdrew slightly on all fronts and a lull came in the fighting. Slone located his field glasses and studied the corpse of the white man. Funny, he didn't dress like a Comanchero. None of them seemed to be. Who would be riding with the Comanches? Although puzzled, he pushed the thought away to fire at five charging warriors who suddenly burst from the distant defile.

"What is all of that shooting?" Lord Anthony Parrish asked Rebecca when she rode back to the wagons for the midday stop.

"I don't know," the lovely girl told him. "Lone Wolf is going to look it over. We won't stop long."

In twenty minutes, Lone Wolf came back to the caravan. "There's about thirty whites pinned down over that distant rise. They are being attacked by Comanches and a few white men," he reported.

"Jake Tulley," Rebecca declared, eyes aglow with the desire to confront her enemy.

"No guarantee of that. It looks bad for the men they have under fire."

"We have weapons enough. Why don't we take the Comanches by surprise?" Rebecca suggested, all the while visualizing Bitter Creek Jake Tulley and his scruffy band of outlaws.

"That's absurd!" Lady Priscilla blurted from her perch on a wagon seat.

"No, it's not," Jason said in support of Rebecca.

"I say, we could be getting into a rather sticky situation, could we not?" Sir Devon inquired.

"Indian warriors do not fight like disciplined white armies. They go into battle as individuals," Rebecca patiently explained. "Mostly it's hit and run tactics. Their leaders have only nominal control. They don't like to take on a larger force than their own and they don't like surprises. It's . . ." she paused a moment. "It's considered bad medicine if things don't go the way they planned it. If we take them by surprise, in the rear, chances are they'll break off and run for it."

"And if they don't?" Lord Anthony drawled.

"It will still give the trapped men a chance to mount up and break out."

"I agree with Lady Priscilla," Sir Devon interposed. "It is entirely too risky. We didn't come here to engage in some foreign war."

"We have to go. It . . . it's sort of like . . ." Rebecca sought the right words. "Like when the hurricane struck our ship. 'The code of the sea,' the captain called it. Those who can help do so and any ship in distress knows that another in sight will come to its rescue, no matter the danger. In any part of the plains where there are hostiles, it is a matter of survival to aid those in trouble."

"No. It isn't our fight," Sir Devon declared.

"You're certainly right, Sir Devon," Priscilla supported him.

"I'm sorry, my dear, but I think you both are wrong. I for one will take my chances with attacking the Indians."

"Anthony!" Lady Priscilla stammered at her husband.

"It's decided, then," Rebecca announced. "Someone has to stay here with Lady Priscilla, Christopher, and the servants. If you are so worried, Sir Devon, you can be the one."

"I for one would like to go," Riggs declared quietly.

"Good man," Rebecca enthused and gave him a peck on the cheek. Usually unflappable, the austere valet blushed a deep red and tenderly placed two fingers on the spot where he had been so energetically bussed.

THIRTEEN

It didn't matter to Captain Slone that the Comanches and their white allies had pulled off and contented themselves with a few sniping rounds from time to time. His command still remained trapped. He consulted a large "turnip" watch he carried in a vest pocket. Two hours and a little over the battle had gone on with all the while more Comanches joining the attack force. There had been few losses on either side, but the reinforcements for the hostiles caused his men to be badly outnumbered. With that many effective fighters, he had no doubt that the Comanches would hold off until nightfall, then sneak up for a night attack. And all he could do was wait.

If only he could get the men mounted. Some distraction that would swing the odds more in their favor. Captain Slone's gaze swept the higher ridge line around the small, bowllike valley in which they had been caught. Several Comanches arrogantly sat their ponies, in plain view, though well out of range, taunting the rangers. Suddenly one of them—a leader to judge by his fancy regalia—jerked from the saddle.

Rebecca Caldwell knelt beside Jason Plumm's prone figure. The British nobleman coolly took aim with his big double rifle. He nodded in satisfaction and picked his first target.

"We all charge after Jason, Lord Anthony and Riggs fire two shots each."

"Is that wise?" Monson asked. "There are so few of us."

"We have to let the Comanches see some sort of force," Rebecca told him. "A few long-range shots could be a single person. What we're gambling on is that the war chief in charge and his councilors will think we are the advance party of a large relief force."

"We have a clear field of fire at a group on the opposite side. We had better do it now," Jason advised her.

One after the other, the three powerful rifles bellowed into the late afternoon stillness.

On the slight rise, overlooking the trapped rangers, Fox sat alert and upright on his pony. He and the others in his wing of the attack had retrieved their mounts after the second charge and withdrawal. Now they waited for the signal for a massive attack that would sweep over the hated rangers and exterminate them. He held his lance in readiness to make the signal. How good it felt to fight the fabled Texas Rangers and, for once, see them on the edge of destruction. His face glowed with the warmth of a certain victory.

His triumphant expression became suddenly marred when a big 480 grain Rigby Match bullet from Jason's Jeffrey double rifle popped a hole under his nose and blew off the back of his head. His corpse flew backward and hit the ground before his followers heard the shot.

In rapid succession, two more warriors toppled from their ponies, bodies twitching in the dust.

Then the heavy boom of the big game rifles rolled over the valley.

"Where did those shots come from?" Jake Tulley asked Sonney Boyle.

"Weren't from the rangers, I can tell you that. Wait a minute." Boyle extended his arm to point to the distant ridge. "Over there. See the smoke?"

"Damn, that's a mighty long shot for anybody. Weren't any Winchester," Tulley surmised. "Maybe a Sharps."

"How many you figure is over there? An' where in hell did they come from?"

"I don't know."

New spurts of smoke powder appeared on the hillside. Jake Tulley watched, open mouthed, as a second later, two more braves fell from their ponies. One Comanche's horse gave a shrill cry, threw its rider and crashed to the ground, blood pouring from its nostrils and mouth.

"By God, that's some shootin'," Jake exclaimed.

"You'd better get down, Jake, before they decide to pick on us." Sonney had already dismounted.

Suddenly a string of riders broke out of the thin

stand of blackjack trees and charged toward the besieged rangers.

"Hey," Harold Prine shouted. "We got help from someone."

Captain Slone had seen the long-range kills and heard the shots. His mind ran in high gear. This could be the diversion he had wanted. "To your horses, boys. We're gonna ride like hell right through those hostiles."

A cheer rose from his men.

At first, Rolling Thunder could not believe what he saw. Fox dead. Big Spotted Cat, too. Had *Karolo's* vision been wrong? What powerful magic did these new whites possess?

He had seen puffs of smoke on the opposite ridge, then a heartbeat later, Fox and two warriors fell from their ponies. Big Spotted Cat and Blue Elk were next. Stone Heart had his pony shot out from under him. Forcefully, Rolling Thunder shook himself from this weak way of thought.

Braves would have to be sent after the men who did this. Buffalo hunters, he judged from the long range. Two, maybe three men, the war chief estimated.

Then he saw a line of riders break from the trees and race toward the trapped rangers. Quickly he counted them.

For so few to charge so recklessly, he reasoned, a large relief force must be close behind. He raised his lance and called to his men.

"Many rangers are coming. We have fought enough this day. Ride in all directions of the wind. We will gather at the camp. Hurry!"

"Where are you goin'?" Jake Tulley shouted as the Comanches around him mounted up and started to gallop away.

"Many heap ranger," Rolling Thunder grunted out in broken English.

"You can't just give it up now. We got 'em beat."

"No. We go. You want stay, you stay," Rolling Thunder declared over his shoulder as he topped the rise and started out of view.

"Goddamnit!" Jake Tulley shouted after the retreating Indians. "Well . . . *goddamnit!*" He swung into the saddle. The sudden desertion by the Comanches left him with no other choice. "Let's ride, boys," he called to his gang.

The rangers charged in the direction from which their rescue came. The few braves caught between the two forces died in a rapid crackle of gunfire. With Captain Slone in the lead, the rugged men of the Frontier Company soon closed with Rebecca's small force.

Captain Slone blinked in surprise to see a woman along. "How many are comin' behind you?" he asked Lone Wolf. "We can run them damned Comanches into the ground."

"We're all there is," Rebecca told him.

"You're . . . what?"

"We took the chance that our unexpected arrival would break off the attack on you. I'm Rebecca Caldwell. This is Bret Baylor, Lord Jason Plumm, Lord Anthony Parrish, Riggs, and Monson."

"By God, young woman, you took one hell of a risk," the ranger captain complimented profanely. "But I have to say I'm glad you did."

"Were there any white men with the Comanches?" Rebecca asked.

Slone's eyes narrowed. "How'd you come to figure that?"

"Then there were?" Rebecca paused a moment, formulating what she would say. "You might find part of this hard to believe. The man leading them is Jake Tulley. Bret and I have been following him from Dakota Territory to New Orleans, and now into Texas. I have . . . very good reasons for wanting to see Tulley dead."

"Too bad you didn't pot him with those long shootin' rifles of yours." Slone looked admiringly at Jason's Jeffrey.

"British made, don't you know," Jason offered as he handed the weapon to the ranger captain. "A Jeffrey. Four-Fifty caliber. Excellent at extended range, though the bullet takes a long time to get there. Actually, I understand, your Sharps is a better rifle."

"Fine weapon," Slone agreed. "But slow. Now, we're fixin' to go after those Comanches. Are you folks of a mind to join us?"

"There are others, Captain, whom we left a few miles away," Jason began.

"Lord Jason and his party are on a hunting expedition," Rebecca added.

"Hunting? With all these damn Comanches on the prowl?" Slone said in wonderment. "Uh . . . then again, I suppose you can take care of yourselves with these big guns."

"Quite," Riggs inserted.

"We have to get back to the rest of the party," Rebecca told the ranger captain. "I'm afraid that would delay you unnecessarily. Perhaps our trails will cross again, Captain."

"I certainly hope so, Miss Caldwell," Slone replied, an appraising twinkle in his eyes. "Maybe we won't be in need of rescue then."

After returning to the waiting wagons, pack animals, and people, the caravan set off on a trail roughly parallel to that taken by the Tulley gang. Rebecca and Lone Wolf had discussed this course of action and agreed to the necessity of not informing Jason and the others of their intentions. The remaining hours of daylight saw them well on their way. They made camp in the gathering twilight, while huge towers of thunderheads built in the southwest.

Jason set to work reloading every expended cartridge while Monson prepared the evening meal. He wasn't entirely convinced that they had seen the last of the Comanches or Rebecca's Jake Tulley. When he completed the task, he walked out onto the prairie and looked around at the impressive emptiness and the powerful display of nature.

Lady Priscilla found him there a few moments later. Lightning flickered in the distant clouds, and the face nearest to them seemed to boil in a turmoil of its own, growing larger as it drew nearer. She placed a hand on his shoulder.

"Jason," she began in a husky voice. "Later tonight, after Tony is asleep, I want to come to your tent."

"You . . . what?"

"I can bear it no longer. I must share your love. Tony sleeps like a stone. He'll never know I am gone. Please, my dearest Jason. Say yes. I . . . I can't live without you."

"Really, Priss. This is . . . so irregular. I can't possibly imagine what gave you the idea . . . I mean, you are a good friend, close to me, certainly. Yet, you are a married woman and . . . well, this sort of thing simply isn't done."

"But it is," she protested. A sharp pang wounded her heart and she tasted the bitter bile of rejection. "Many married women take . . . amaratos. As we approach a certain point in life, we find we need . . . something beyond the humdrum existence of home and husband. I've hungered for you since you were a mere lad of fifteen. Please, Jason. I'm offering you everything. We can be discreet, cautious. You can't deny me."

Jason patted her cheek fondly. "I'm flattered, of course. But I can and I do deny any such assignation for us. It would be . . . dishonorable."

As before, rejection turned from sorrow to anger. Lady Priscilla slapped Jason stingingly on the cheek and stormed off into a dry wash.

A long moment went by while Jason gently touched his burning cheek. Then he heard a rustle in the dry grass behind him. He turned to see Anthony approaching.

"I must say, old boy, you're a gentleman of the old school," Anthony drawled. "I mean every bit of that. I, ah, happened to observe Priscilla's scandalous proposition. I'd like to apologize for her. Your sportsmanship and fair play have been a source of envy on my part for some time."

"Why . . . I . . ."

Anthony held up a hand. "No, no. Let me finish. I am well aware that my wife has had numerous, ah, affairs. Some of them not so flattering as a peer of the realm. Stable boys, that sort of tawdry thing. I admire you for your fortitude and your denouement that such conduct would be dishonorable. A man like you I value as a friend. I'm sorry this all happened, Jason. Here's my hand on it."

They shook solemnly while thunder blasted open the sky.

"Now, if you will excuse me, I'm going after my wife. It's time we had a serious talk about all this."

Anthony Parrish followed his wife's path off into the wash. Another sound came to Jason's ears then. Closer and more ominous than the thunder, he heard a roar that reminded him of a great cataract.

The sound was only too familiar to Rebecca Caldwell. She came running toward Jason and called out to him. "Flash flood. Is anyone down in that creek bed?"

"Pris and Tony," Jason answered back. Only then did he understand her meaning.

The next instant, Priscilla screamed.

FOURTEEN

A tremendous gust of wind tore at Rebecca's hair as she ran past Jason. Suddenly the sky above opened and dumped sheets of water down on them. Lady Priscilla screamed again. Rebecca turned her head from side to side to locate the source of the sound.

By then the churning flood waters bore down on where she and Jason stood on the bank. Mud, rocks, and chunks of tree limbs tumbled in the leading edge of the deluge. Close to the near edge, Rebecca saw a slender, pale white arm and hand.

"There she is." Rebecca leaped in and grabbed onto Lady Priscilla's wrist. With her free hand, she anchored the two of them to an exposed cottonwood root.

A moment later, Jason located Anthony, spinning in a miniature whirlpool. He dived in and swam across the surge of water with powerful strokes. He clutched Anthony by a foot and pushed on toward the opposite bank. Lightning struck nearby, the odor of ozone overwhelming as the murderous crash of sound assaulted everyone's ears. Another ten feet and he would find purchase on the bank, Jason gauged. He increased his efforts.

Within a minute, Rebecca dragged a sodden Lady Priscilla free of the raging stream. The dripping British peer sputtered a moment, jerked free of Rebecca's grasp, and stalked away without a word of thanks or an expression of concern for her husband. Rebecca saw Jason pull Anthony free of the water on the far bank and turned back to camp.

Wind and driving rain had caused considerable damage. The fire, of course, was out. A two foot square chunk of canvas, all that remained of the shelter under which they took their meals, flapped in the bluster with a sound like gunshots. Rebecca found everyone crowded into the wagons to escape the storm. The flimsy partitions kept out rain and, though rocked by ferocious gusts, they remained upright. The first wagon she sought shelter in, Rebecca came eye to eye with Lady Priscilla. Hatred blazed like lightning and Becky spun away to the more congenial atmosphere of the other wagon.

Gradually the torrent slackened, the wind moderated, and the storm moved on across the prairie. The members of the expedition stepped out onto the muddy ground, and Rebecca assured them that Jason and Anthony had come through safely. Then she noticed someone else missing from the gathering.

"Has anyone seen Chris?" she asked, a worried tone in her voice.

"He, ah, went out to answer a call of nature, Miss Rebecca," Riggs offered. "I had assumed he returned and took shelter in the other wagon."

*　　　*　　　*

Christopher lowered his trousers and squatted, using a large rock for a support. He had barely begun to rid himself of the pressure in his bowels when he heard a rumbling, closer and louder than the thunder. Even through the thick soles of his shoes he could feel a growing vibration in the ground. Memory of the buffalo stampede assured him he was in imminent danger. Before he could rise and fasten his trousers, he saw a black wall, its upper surface flecked with white foam, hurtle around a curve in the creek bed and race toward him.

Its gurgling roar identified it to him as water. Suddenly it slammed over him, grinding the small body along its bed, then tumbling and spinning him to the surface. The boy was working on his second gasp of sweet air when the turbulence snatched him under again. Got to swim, Christopher thought frantically. He kicked free of his shoes and shed his trousers, working against tremendous pressure. At last, rid of these encumbrances, he surged to the surface.

The world seemed to whirl around him. He sucked in deep draughts of air and tried to recognize any familiar objects in the close-spaced flashes of lightning. His ears rang from the constant cannonading of the thunder, and his strength ebbed as he tried to fight the current. At last he managed to control his frantic body and forced himself to swim in slow strokes, barely expending enough energy to keep his head above water. The thick trunk of a cottonwood, uprooted by the flood, appeared in front of him.

With every ounce of his vitality, the slender boy stroked through the water until he caught his makeshift raft. He clung to it with all his might and let the raging torrent take him where it wished.

He must have gone a mile, Christopher thought, when he saw, in a lightning flash, a white crescent of sandbar sticking up above the flood. When the next blaze of electric fury came, he oriented himself to the sprit and pushed off from his log. He used short, chopping strokes to propel himself through the water. A trick of current sent the cottonwood swinging his way in a vicious arc. Desperately he dived under the surface.

Deeper. He had to go deeper, the youngster thought, as he tried to force himself to the bottom of the wash. Pebbles scraped his extended fingers and he clung to the insecure anchorage with both hands as the tree swept over him. He felt pain in one leg and realized the rough bark had scraped his left calf. When his lungs could bear it no longer, Christopher pushed off and streaked for the surface.

The next lightning flash showed that the incident with the tree had taken him past his refuge. What could he do now? At this point the swimming was easier. He set out for the left bank and nearly reached the exposed roots of a tree when a treacherous current swept him back toward the more turbulent water in mid-stream. The minutes dragged by in his watery world. Lightning sizzled through the sodden air once more and, at a bend ahead, he saw the cause of his troubles grounded on an even larger sandbar. Safety at last, he congratulated himself.

Rested now, Christopher swam with strong, smooth strokes until his toes dug into sand. Faint with relief he dragged himself onto the damp beach. He lay on his belly, gasping and choking on the taste of the flood water. At last he slowly sat up. His legs and arms ached, and so did his stomach. Every muscle felt as though it had been stretched beyond endurance and then let go slack. The rain decreased and he shivered in the cold wind that whipped against his sodden clothing. After a moment he fought to choke back a sob. Here he was, he knew not where, half naked—the lower half at that—without shoes or food or any means of signaling. Besides that, blood still oozed from the raw scrape on his left calf. What could he possibly do?

A star peeped through the cloud cover and the rain quit altogether. In ten minutes, by Christopher's estimate, the sky cleared and the wind died down. Cheered by this, Christopher tore a long swath from his shirt and crudely bandaged his leg. He checked his surroundings and climbed, limping, up the sandbar. On the shoreward side, a sea of sludge and slimy water separated him from the bank. He heard a thrashing in the water behind him and hurried back to the swiftly moving creek.

Trapped in twisted branches of the cottonwood, a half-drowned rabbit struggled feebly to get free. Christopher fell on it in delight. At least he would have food of a sort. He tore another strip from his shirt tail to make a snare that would hold his prize, then sat down to study the stars.

Wet, cold, and alone, Christopher waited through the night.

FIFTEEN

When the swift current had subsided and the water level dropped to waist level, Jason brought Anthony back to camp. Then he learned that Christopher was missing and organized an immediate search, despite the weather.

Although the search had continued through most of the night, nothing had been found of Christopher. Lady Priscilla, Rebecca noted, seemed little concerned by the evident tragedy. Jason was nearly frantic. Even though he had yet to be married, Jason had a father's instinct toward the boy. Where Christopher's father remained aloof and untouchable in the halls of Parliament and the youngster removed from his home in a boarding school, Jason saw him often and lavished affection on him. Now he faced the awful possibility that the flash flood had claimed Christopher's life. At his worried insistence, the search resumed at first light.

The need for security dictated the make-up of the search party. Issac and Cootyarkey, the Delaware guides, set out to scout for signs of the Comanche or Tulley's evil band. The waters had receded and Lone Wolf, along with Riggs, searched the near bank, while Rebecca and Jason crossed over to take the far side. Slowly they moved downstream, pausing to minutely examine each clump of flotsam that had snagged along the way. With each negative discovery, their hopes faltered.

From miles beyond their site, millions of gallons of runoff had poured into the creek, which roughly followed the path of the violent storm. Feeding on itself like that, it had reached a tumultuous stage by the time it swept past the campsite. Christopher's body could have been washed all the way to the North Fork of the Red River, Issac had suggested before riding out to the west. Painfully aware of this possibility, the searchers made their way farther from camp.

Abruptly, nearly a mile and a half from the wagons, Rebecca halted Ike and turned to Jason. Her highly developed sense of smell had detected an odor that had no business there.

"Jason, do you smell that?"

Plumm sniffed the air. "What? I don't notice anything in particular."

"Someone is cooking meat near here. Come on."

Two hundred yards farther on, Rebecca spied a thin tendril of blue-white smoke rising from below the bank rim. She stopped again.

"I smell it now," Jason said excitedly. "Could it be . . . Christopher's alive?"

"Yes. Or it might be some of Tulley's men. They aren't all that trail wise and could be cooking this close to our camp. We had better move quietly."

They took ten minutes to cover the next three hundred yards. The smoke had become more visible now, rising from only a few feet away. Rebecca dismounted, drew one of her Smith and Wesson .44 Americans, and crawled through the waving buffalo grass to the lip of the bank. Cautiously she peered over at the scene below.

On a sandbar, some forty feet from the bank, she saw two crude frameworks of broken branches. They held a shirt and wool jacket, drying near a small fire. Over the low blaze, a rabbit carcass turned on a green stick, held in place by forked uprights and tended by a very naked Christopher Anderson.

Even from that distance, the boy's pale, untanned body showed signs of scratches and bruises and, when he stood to get more wood, a nasty scrape on his left calf. Rebecca prolonged her observation until the youngster returned to the fire. She wanted to make certain that the boy wasn't being used as a decoy to lure them into a trap.

Satisfied, when she found no sign of Comanches or Tulley's men lurking about, she crawled backward a bit, rose and walked quickly to Jason, a smile lighting her lovely features.

"It's Chris, all right. He's cooking himself a rabbit for breakfast. His clothes are drying by the fire and he's in his ah, all-together. Doesn't seem the least concerned about his condition."

"I say! Is . . . is he all right?"

"A few cuts and such. Over all, I'd say he looks rather good." Her impish grin conveyed a rather lurid image to Jason.

"Really. He's only a boy."

"I know that. You still looked so tense I thought a little teasing might loosen you up."

"Let's go get him."

"There's about forty feet of mudhole and backwater between us and the bar."

"Humm. How do we do it?"

151

"I'd say we ride down stream a little, get to the bottom of the bank and call to him. The water is low enough now that Chris can carry his clothes and wade to where we are."

"If we both go down there, it might embarrass him to death."

"I can stay behind," Rebecca offered.

"Actually I was thinking it the other way around. Sort of like his mother, or his nanny, you know?"

"Not, ah, really."

"Well, then, we'll both go."

Two minutes later, the pair started down the steep creek bank. An undercut portion of the clay-laden soil let go without warning and left Jason stranded for the moment, able only to go upward.

"I'll find another place and join you soon," he advised.

Rebecca went on. "Chris!" she called when she came within sight of the boy. "Christopher, it's me, Rebecca."

Excitedly, forgetting his circumstances, Christopher rose and turned toward the voice. "Oh, Miss Rebecca, I'm so glad to see you. I . . ." Suddenly he blushed from the roots of his hair to the tips of his toes. He uttered a startled little squeak and turned sideways, hands shielding his groin.

"I . . . I'm terribly sorry . . ." he stammered.

"Nothing to worry about. The Sioux bathe in the nude, regardless of age or sex. They go swimming that way, too. In five years I saw a great number of unclothed boys. We want to get you back to camp, so please hurry. Gather your clothes and wade over to me. The water shouldn't be more than knee deep for you. You can dress once we get to the top of the bank."

"I . . . what about my hare? I'd very much like to eat him, now that I caught him and prepared him, don't you see?"

Rebecca laughed. "Bring him along then. Breakfast when we get back to the wagons."

Christopher took a deep breath, put aside his hesitancy and moved about the sandbar, gathering his few possessions. Lastly he lifted the smoking rabbit from the fire and, brandishing it like a banner, stepped into the water. Without any show of self-consciousness, he floundered through the chilly stream to where Rebecca waited, as though unaware of his nakedness. When he reached the small mud-and-sand shelf at the base of the bank, he laid his clothing over an exposed root of a washed away cottonwood, propped the rabbit against it, and hugged Rebecca around the middle, his cheek pressed against her bosom. After a moment, he stepped back, eyes shining.

"This is the second time you've saved my life, Miss Rebecca. I . . . I've grown to love you very much," he managed before he trailed off in stammering embarrassment.

"We had better get to the top so you can cover some of your, ah, more obvious emotions."

Christopher blushed again, then picked up his burdens and started the ascent. As they climbed, he chattered on about adventure. Jason greeted them at the top as he reached his story of the rabbit.

"I saw this hare caught in the washed up branches," he began after he had embraced his uncle and exchanged expressions of gratitude for his safety. "I caught it and made a snare of a strip from my shirt. This morning I found some dry wood, used the flint and steel in my jacket pocket to start a fire, than set about drying my clothes. By then my shirt had suffered a bit," he went on as he shrugged into the ragged-hemmed garment. It ended an inch above his navel.

"I wrung the hare's neck, skinned and cleaned it.

153

Then I made a spit and started roasting my breakfast. I had no idea, you see, how long I might be there. That's when you came along." The boy shrugged into his damp jacket. "I lost my shoes and trousers in the flood, I'm afraid."

"If you hadn't shed them, chances are you would have drowned," Rebecca reassured him. She fired two rounds from the .44 to notify Lone Wolf that Christopher had been found.

"Up you go," Jason told him, indicating his mount. "It's time we got back to the others."

"I . . . ah . . . might I ride with Miss Rebecca, please, sir?" Christopher begged his uncle, the light of his infatuation glowing in his gray-blue eyes.

Rebecca and Jason exchanged glances and burst out laughing. For the life of him, Christopher could not imagine why.

Jake Tulley took the pint whiskey bottle from his lips and hurled it against a large rock. The thick, profile likeness of George Washington, molded into the glass, shattered into a thousand shards that sparkled in the sunlight.

"Damn that girl!" he exploded.

"What?" Roger Styles asked offhandedly.

"Rebecca Caldwell. I saw her, I tell you. White doeskin dress, braids and all. It was she and that white savage she pards with that led the relief to the rangers. I want to go back and get her."

"Are you out of your mind?"

They had made a separate camp, a long distance from Rolling Thunder's valley, in order not to be taken by surprise. Roger had been certain the rangers would follow up the Comanches and locate their village. It wouldn't do to be caught in such a situation. With rangers riding all over the area and a force of undetermined size, with or without Rebecca Caldwell hunting them, it would be suicide to head out in search of trouble.

"No. I mean it. We've got Wild Horse's warriors not far away. That scout he sent with us could reach them in no time. Combined with my boys, we can take on whatever that vixen has and then lay low until the rangers have to go back to Lubbock."

"You are way out on a limb, Jake. *Nis-ti-u-na* has only fifteen braves. We're down to eleven men. Think it through."

"I have been. I tell you, Roger, we can do it."

"No. We can keep someone on our backtrail. If they spot the rangers, or this other group, we will have warning in time to do something about it. Otherwise it would be throwing good men away for no reason."

"Roger," Jake growled. Hoofbeats interrupted his response.

A scruffy man in floppy hat and buckskins rode into camp. Thin wisps of scalp locks blew in the breeze from his shirt fringe and pocket flaps. He dismounted, whipped off his hat and addressed Roger.

"Heard you had a run-in with the rangers," he began. "I come from Alex Horning and Pablo Gonzales. They wanted you to know that they have thought it over and have decided to join your plan. Their men will be ready to ride at an hour's notice."

"By God!" Jake exploded. "With a dozen or so of them, we've got that Rebecca Caldwell by the balls."

Roger cocked an eyebrow at Jake's rather odd metaphor. But then, he considered, perhaps it fit. In the past, Rebecca Caldwell had shown considerably more

155

balls than the man he had selected to lead the gang. When confronted by her implacable desire for revenge, Jake had often performed no better than the worst bungler. Even her uncle, Ezekiel Caldwell, had gone into hiding. He waited for word from them to come out of his lair in Kansas.

"How about it, Roger? Doesn't this make a difference?"

Reluctantly, Roger had to admit that it did. "How soon could you bring say . . . fifteen men here?"

"Noon tomorrow."

"Fine. Tell Mr. Horning and *Señor* Gonzales we have a deal."

"These are beaded with an Oglala woman's design," Rebecca told Christopher a few minutes before the caravan was ready to roll again. "But that shouldn't make any difference out here. My feet are small, so these moccasins should fit you comfortably."

Christopher pressed the sturdy elk-hide moccasins to his thin chest. "I'd be glad to wear them, no matter what," he told her, his adolescent crush making his voice sound strange and dreamlike.

Once mounted, the small column moved out.

Before he went forward to scout, Lone Wolf came to Rebecca. "Coot says there is an abandoned Spanish mission not far ahead. We should reach it by tomorrow night."

"That would make a good place for Jason to headquarter for his serious hunting," she speculated. "We could leave them there and get on with the search for Tulley."

"Are you certain now is the time for that?"

"Couldn't be any better. Jake Tulley was with those Comanches. I didn't see him but you can bet he got a description of you and me. He could very well have men out looking for us. That would put all these people in grave danger. We'll leave them and hunt for Tulley alone. Once we find him, we can decide how to go about it. We could even call in the rangers if he has too many men."

"Yes. After that ambush, I'm sure Captain Slone has a few questions to ask. The gang may not be wanted in Texas, but that attack yesterday changes things."

"Then we'll do it that way?" Rebecca asked, suddenly sorrowful that in so short a time she would be saying good-bye forever to Jason Plumm.

"Might as well," Lone Wolf agreed.

Rebecca went off to find Jason and inform him of this intelligence.

Once on the trail, Jason and Rebecca rode together, with Christopher not far away. The young lord noticed his nephew's sideways glances filled with longing and smiled at the beautiful girl beside him.

"Chris is madly smitten with you," he commented.

"Yes. It's . . . sort of touching. He is a sweet boy."

"Not that much of a *boy* anymore," Jason prompted.

"Un-huh. I noticed . . . down at the sandbar."

"You have a naughty mind."

"And a roving eye. He, ah, takes after his uncle."

"Shameless!" Jason laughed. "I never thought I'd be jealous of a twelve-year-old."

"You needn't be." She placed a hand over her heart. "I solemnly promise I will not seduce the child."

They chuckled together over that and a few minutes later, Rebecca surveyed the horizon and spoke again. "Let's go find some game for supper," she urged. They spurred their mounts forward, each of them anticipat-

157

ing the secret pleasures the afternoon might bring.

Monson prepared the evening meal as a sort of celebration for Christopher's safe return. Rebecca and Jason had come upon a large covey of quail. Jason's fine, German-made *Schienendrilling*—a 10-gauge double shotgun under a rifle barrel designed for the 10.8x47 Martini cartridge—brought down enough plump birds to provide a brace for everyone, deliciously prepared in a sauce of marsala wine, terragon, and buffalo fat. Rebecca had bagged an excellent Javalina sow, which roasted to a crisp over an open fire. They had it with potatoes, fried, as the superb chef put in, "in the French manner," and wild onions grilled over the coals. Monson even outdid himself by producing a cake.

"A bit of trifle for young Master Christopher," he announced diffidently when he presented the confection.

"A bit more of the claret for everyone," Jason commanded Basil. "I have an announcement."

Basil moved effortlessly around the joined tables, filling wine glasses. When he finished, Jason rose and surveyed the party. "I have been informed by Rebecca that our base camp for the expedition is only a day away. A collection of buildings left behind by the Spanish papists. An old mission, as a matter of fact. So, here's to our hunting headquarters."

Everyone drank and Jason raised his glass again. "Also, to our marvelous friends who have brought us safely through all travails to this promising location. From now on, we shall pursue the wily game in peaceful surroundings."

SIXTEEN

Under a bright, clear blue sky, the cavalcade set out an hour after sunrise the next morning. Their new course tended even further eastward, while still gaining ground to the north. Despite the recent rain, dust soon began to churn up under the wheels of the wagons. The Delaware and Lone Wolf ranged ahead and to the sides and each mile gave a greater sense of security to everyone.

A little before noon, two riders stopped at the old campsite beside the creek. They dismounted and looked around.

"Thes's the ones we're lookin' for, all right. See them narrah wagon wheel tracks?"

"Cain't be more than ten, twelve people, Toby," Sonney Boyle remarked as he studied the footprints in the drying prairie soil.

"Yeah. But they got them long-range rifles. D'you see that yesterday?"

"See it? They damned near killed me."

"We gonna go back and tell Jake?"

"Naw. We'll push on until we catch sight of 'em. Can't be goin' too fast with those wagons."

"Ain't headin' the same direction," the young gunslick observed. "Turned farther east."

"Yep," Boyle agreed. "Well, we'd best be about it."

By mid-afternoon, the heat, abetted by increased humidity, made the day oppressive enough to resemble summer. The wagon teams drooped their heads and plodded along, visions of cool water and oats in their dim brains. The scouts had drawn closer in to the convoy, directing it toward the distant mission grounds.

Unseen by the travelers, Sonney Boyle and his companion watched from a ravine, moving when their quarry dropped out of sight over a swell. At last, Sonney sent Toby Waters ahead to determine where the caravan might stop. After the gunslick departed, Sonney spent two hours skirting the trail, observing everything about the strange party.

At last Toby returned. "There's an old, rundown bunch of adobe buildings a ways from here. Looks like they can make it there by evening."

Sonney thought on it for a while, then swung into the saddle. "Let's go report to Jake. The Comancheros oughta be in by the time we get there."

"Thought they was supposed to made it by noon."

"Down in this country, there's more'n one speed to tell time by. Could be, they won't show until midnight. There's a bunch of greasers with that outfit. They move slow."

Long bars of red lay on the western horizon, shot through with vertical shafts of purple by the time

160

Sonney and Toby reached Jake's camp. They dismounted, gratefully took a slug from an offered whiskey bottle, and went to make their report.

Roger and Jake listened to each word, asked a few questions, and sent for the leader of the Comanchero detachment. "Looks like we can eliminate one big problem, maybe two," Jake began when the strategy meeting convened. "'Course it'll require a long ride durin' the night. Even then, when we get there, they might have gone on. All the same, we catch the Caldwell girl an' them others at the old mission or on the trail, we can wipe 'em out to the last person. Sonney, you send someone to fetch ol' Wild Horse and his braves. We got a lot of killin' for 'em to do."

The Spanish had planned their mission grounds with a thought to defend against hostile tribes. A high wall, broken to waist level in some points by age and weather, surrounded the compound. A weathered and rickety wooden platform ran around all four sides near the top. Broken glass and sharp, jagged bits of metal, now rusted to uselessness, had been set into the upper surface of the parapet to repel attackers. The buildings had fared better than the wall.

A long, low dormitory of narrow rooms ran along one side. Cells for the monastic order who had operated the mission. A dining hall lay ruined in melted lumps of adobe, though the separated kitchen remained in excellent condition. An adobe foundation marked out the site of a large barn, though the wooden upper portions had been burned away. Another structure, probably a post house, or *posada*, for travelers, stretched along another wall, complete with a small bar on the lower floor. The chapel remained intact, except for the roof of the vestry, which gaped open at the prairie sky. It would, everyone decided after a brief inspection, serve admirably as a headquarters.

Monson and Basil got busy in the kitchen while Lady Priscilla staked out quarters in the posada. She issued a string of demands for bedding, heavy trunks containing her clothing, and other items from the wagons. Everyone else selected rooms, with at least the semblance of beds in them. Dinner, Monson announced, would be served in the taproom of the inn, rather than the usual *al fresco* arrangement under a canvas shelter. Christopher padded around in his moccasins, gathering firewood for the cook stove and enjoying the feeling of freedom the lightweight elk-hide shoes gave his bare feet. The entire party seemed more relaxed than since their departure from San Angelo.

All except Rebecca. She paced the usable portions of the parapet platform and gazed intently out over the rolling plains. "I feel it somehow," she confided to Lone Wolf. "Jake Tulley is out there somewhere, headed our way."

"Don't let your imagination get the best of you," he cautioned. "He could be miles from here, or even on his way out of Texas. Not even Jake Tulley is stupid enough to sit around and invite the attentions of the rangers."

Rebecca shrugged. "Perhaps you're right. Even so, I think it would be wise to post a watch tonight."

"I suppose so. Too bad that well has gone bad. Though we have plenty of water and the creek is within safe distance from the walls."

"Thinking about an attack, too?"

"I don't like to admit it, but, yes. It's wise to consider all possibilities."

"You live longer that way," Rebecca agreed.

*   *   *

An early-rising moon had set and the tablelands of the Panhandle softly glowed under a dazzling wash of stars. Rebecca, her clothes in a heap beside her, sat on a blanket, her back cushioned by another against the bole of an ancient olive tree, planted by long dead Franciscan friars as a reminder of their homeland. Her breath came in short, jerky gasps, one sharp intake with each thrust of Jason's facile tongue.

He knelt between her wide-spread legs, which glowed pale bronze in the starlight, and dedicated full attention to the delectable banquet presented to him. While he probed the intriguing folds of her rosy cleft, his lips gently nuzzled its outer surface. He used rapid, circular motions to stimulate the hot, rigidly distended protrusion that nestled in the upper arch of this delightful crevice and his nostrils flared at the heady aroma of her womanly elixir that emanated from her vibrant channel. When Rebecca's gasps changed to a steady keening, he swiftly brought her to a raging peak, then ceased his ministrations, so that she became suspended momentarily in a limbo of exquisite sensation.

With practiced skill, he repositioned the lovely girl and lowered himself between her silken thighs. With one mightly shove, he drove his rigid phallus to the hilt in her moist, palpitating furnace like a diver entering a deep pool. Rebecca gave a strangled cry and arched upward to receive every possible bit of that marvelous gift and clung to its fullness with tightened muscles. For a moment they trembled like youngsters in their first encounter, the nerve-fraying totality of their shared pleasure enfolding them in a sensual oblivion. The held like this for as long as it could be endured. Then, with long, slow strokes, Jason began to plumb the richness of her inner being.

"I . . . am . . . a . . . horrid . . . wanton . . . woman," Rebecca grunted out past the block passion had placed in her throat.

"The best I've ever known, darling," Jason murmured in her ear. His tongue searched the circular passages inside it while he raised slightly and swayed his pelvis in delightful orbits, while fully encased by her gently pulling purse. It sent shivers of delicious excitement through them both.

"Oh ... yes ... yes ... like that ... more ... harder ... AAAAH!" Rebecca panted in a high, tremulous voice.

Images swirled in her wildly stimulated brain. She saw herself as a young girl, bathing in the creek near the Caldwell homestead in northern Nebraska. A hand strayed to her hairless mound and a tingle spread through her body as she inserted a finger. Then, suddenly, inexplicably, Four Horns was with her, his long, rigid penis poking out from his body, pressing against her lower belly, demanding, hungry. Her own delightful madness flushed her with desire and she reached for that throbbing cylinder of flesh, encircled it and began to stroke, guided by nature rather than experience. The image changed and she saw many faces, many positions and beds, carpets and widespread trees. Most dominant, though, was the face that hovered over her now. The clean, strong lines, prominent, acquiline nose and jutting chin. How beloved it was!

"Jason! Oh, Jason!" she exclaimed in a shuddering voice. "Faster ... faster ... now ... oh ... NOW." With a wild wail, she crashed over the peak and sped down into eternity.

Deftly, Jason paced himself and worked them both into a frenzy as he ascended toward the pinnacle of the little death. With joyful abandon, they surrendered to it together.

"You're good for me," Jason whispered once they had returned to sanity and the real world. "There is no reason why we should not . . ."

Rebecca placed two fingers on his lips. "Please, Jason . . ."

"No. Listen to me," he went on with determination. "I've mentioned my estates and such lightly so far. Now, it is necessary that you understand. I am, by American standards, really quite wealthy. My estates aren't exactly a large plantation or two. It's the better part of a small county in the midlands. Two villages, seventeen farms, a rather nice wood with deer and game birds. There are orchards, two dairies, sheep, cattle, a tannery, woolen mills. We have something to do with foreign trade. Sir Devon could tell you more about that. I am single, never married, twenty-four years old, in good health and," he paused and chuckled softly, "as you can attest, not at all incapable of being ardent. In short, the perfect formula for a suitable husband.

"Now, were I to marry someone not of my class, I would not be compelled to surrender my estates or my title. But . . . oh, my dearest Rebecca, even if I had to, I would gladly do so if only you would consent to be my wife. I'd throw it all over and move to America if you wanted it."

"Jason . . . I . . ." Tears formed in Rebecca's deep blue eyes and rolled silently down her cheeks. "You know about me. About my past. And yet you . . . you want me as a wife? I . . . I don't know what to say."

"It's a simple word. Say, 'yes.'"

"I . . . can't. It isn't that easy. You thrill me in more ways and more completely than anyone ever has. Not just the physical. You are strong, decisive, forceful. You are rich and adventurous. All the things that fit so

165

perfectly into my life. It would be so easy to accept. I *want* to accept. Still, there remains the specter of Jake Tulley."

"To hell with Jake Tulley," Jason growled. "I want you for my wife."

"And I want revenge. How can I put it? No matter how deeply I desire you, no matter how perfect our lovemaking, I feel somehow . . . incomplete until I see the last one of those scum die before my eyes.

"You can have no idea what it is like to be fourteen years old and have part of you ache to explore the mysteries of sex while the other part lives in constant terror of being gang-raped by fifty Oglala warriors and every boy in camp old enough to get it up. There were other captives in Iron Calf's village. I saw what happened to them. Some, younger than I was, endured a man or boy lusting inside them five and six times a day."

"Easy, my darling. All that is behind you."

"No. It is as real as those stars above us. As real as the warmth of your body beside me. Jake Tulley and my uncles put me in the way of that sort of treatment. If it hadn't been that I was Iron Calf's daughter, it would have happened. I killed my Uncle Virgil. I can't rest, I can't be myself until I do the same to Tulley and Uncle Ezekiel."

"I can change your mind," Jason murmured, his hands busy teasing her body to new raptures.

"Oh, yes. I'm afraid you can. I . . . yes, there. Rub it. It shoots off stars in my head. Aaah, Jason, Jason. That's it . . . that's really it!"

At her direction, Jason lay on his back and she straddled him. Slowly, with all the art of a tease, she lowered herself, taking a tiny half inch of him at a time into the liquid-bathed tunnel that pulsed and contracted around his slender, throbbing shaft.

Words forgotten for the moment, they made joyful, energetic love long into the night.

The crack of a .44-40 slug striking the wall above her head awakened Rebecca a few minutes after sunrise.

Outside, the Delaware guides' rifles spoke in defiance and Cootyarkey yelled down from the wall. "We're being attacked. Everyone up!"

Rebecca hurried from her bed and slid into her doeskin dress. Her body vibrated with a pleasant ache that reminded her of the wonderful night just passed. She grabbed up her heavy brace of Smith and Wesson .44s and rushed outside.

One half of the large, double gates remained on its hinges. It had been swung into place by Lone Wolf. Jason Plumm and Sir Devon shoved one of the wagons into the gap left by the burned-down portion. Behind them, Anthony Parrish, Riggs, and Christopher struggled with the second vehicle. Rebecca reached the wall in time to fire point-blank at a screaming Comanche.

Her slug caught him high in the breastbone, snapped back his head and cleaned him off his charging pony, to fall in the path of those behind. Then she had time to take in the situation.

Out about a hundred and fifty yards, a dozen scruffy-looking men, whites and Mexicans, sat their mounts and fired rifles at the defenders. As the Comanches whirled away and raced back to form another charge, the roughly dressed men kicked their heels into their animals' sides and thundered toward the wall. More whites, among them, she recognized, Opie Dillon, took their place and began to shoot. The Tulley gang had showed itself at last, she thought expectantly as she returned fire.

Bullets cracked through the air and thudded into the thick, plaster-covered adobe wall. One round caromed off the top of the parapet and moaned through the air until it struck the bell in the church tower. The aged, cracked tocsin gave off an eerie clangor.

The second charge neared the wall. Rebecca took careful aim and squeezed the trigger of a .44 American. The muzzle jumped and smoke spurted out, obscuring her vision for a moment. Without pause she shifted her position and lined up on another target.

Her second shot sent a bullet into the chest of a lanky man with drooping mustache and close-set, beady eyes. It clipped a wisp of hair from the scalp lock tied to his shirt pocket before it thumped into flesh and sent shards of rib bone into his lung and heart. The big slug clipped the top arch of his aorta and a high pressure spew of blood flooded his upper cavity.

These men are Comancheros, Rebecca realized from a description she had heard earlier. The feared renegades who traded with the hostile Comanches and often negotiated ransom for captives. As they wheeled away in turn, she looked up into the rapidly approaching face of Jake Tulley.

Icily calm, Rebecca took careful aim. A hot slug smacked into the parapet in front of her and showered her eyes with grainy plaster. Tears formed to ease the irritating matter that stung her face and blinded her vision. Compelled by the unexpected torment, she bent low to wipe her smarting eyes.

By the time she stood upright again, Tulley and his nine men had swung away and the Comanches charged again.

"Damn!" she cursed aloud.

In the distance, over three hundred yards from the besieged mission, one Comanchero suddenly threw his arms wide and catapulted over his horse's head. Below

168

her, Jason had put his long range Jeffrey into use.

Two Comanches swung in close to the mission, let fire-arrows fly and started to whirl away. A blast from one barrel of a ten-gauge Drilling splashed one's back with crimson and popped two buckshot holes in the other's head. Riggs opened the breech, removed the expended shell, and blew into the tube before reloading. He snapped the three-barreled weapon into battery and took aim. This time the .45-70 rifle barrel fired and blasted another Comanchero out of the saddle.

Dead before he hit the ground, the renegade's body rebounded into the air, only to disappear under the churning hoofs of his companions' horses. Anthony Parrish fired his Farquharson with deadly accuracy. A Comanche's head exploded in a spray of blood and brain matter. Then, swiftly, the enemy galloped out of range.

"They have gone!" Lady Priscilla shouted from a second floor window of the inn. "We must run for our lives."

"They haven't gone that far," Lone Wolf called back. "We can't go and we're in a bad situation to stay."

"They'll be back," Rebecca added.

Time dragged through half an hour. Then hoofbeats sounded from an unexpected direction. Comanche warriors raced toward the back wall of the compound, firing and screeching their war cries.

A moment later, the Comancheros charged the front gate. The defenders fired with speed and accuracy, yet the attackers pressed on. A third wave, Jake Tulley and his men, came pounding over the flat prairie toward an undefended portion of the walls.

"Over there," Rebecca shouted as she triggered a round in Tulley's direction. She missed, but creased the flank of the horse behind.

A pain-driven shriek came from the wounded animal. It reared and dumped its rider onto the ground. Dust rose and charging horses churned the ground around the fallen man. He screamed in terror and raised his hands frantically to find rescue on the back of another outlaw's mount.

Such succor failed to materialize for him, and he went down in a hailstorm of buckshot from Riggs' Drilling. From the back wall, a trio of Comanches released fire-arrows. They smoked through the air and landed in the roof of the posada. The ancient, weathered beams burst into ready, crackling flames.

"Everybody out of the inn," Rebecca shouted over the tumult of battle. "The roof is on fire. Get out!"

A shriek of anguish came from Lady Priscilla's room. The flames had eaten through and licked hungrily at the furniture below. Lord Anthony abandoned his position on the wall long enough to run inside to bring out his wife.

"Into the church," Rebecca commanded. "Take water, lots of it. Food, Monson," she called to the chef who manned a European rifle at the makeshift barricade in the open gate.

Support timbers fell into the inferno of the inn.

"We'll hold the wall as long as we can," Lone Wolf yelled. "Get to the church. Bring all weapons, ammunition, food, and water you can carry. Hurry."

A Comanche stood on his horse's back like a circus rider. As it thundered in close to the wall he flexed his knees and leaped upward.

His face lost its triumphant leer as his hands slapped down on the shards of broken glass. A screech of agony tore from his lips and he slowly slid out of sight, leaving behind long, wet trails of red. On the ground at the base of the wall, he hugged his lacerated hands to his belly and bent over them moaning.

His misery ended in the blast of Rebecca's .44. The

slug slammed into the top of his head and ripped apart his brain before exiting out through his larynx.

"My clothes. My beautiful clothes," Lady Priscilla wailed as she ran behind her husband across the compound. She staggered under the weight of a huge water cask and nearly fell when her toe connected with the lip of the bottom step in front of the church.

Sudden quiet descended on the scene of fury.

"They've pulled back," Riggs shouted. "On all sides."

Once more the long range rifles opened up, while everyone else set to moving supplies into the church. With one man stationed on each wall, the enemy was kept at bay through the long morning.

"Get everything settled in there," Lone Wolf advised. "Barricade the windows and have something heavy to block every door."

"Once you have the church prepared, we will man the walls until they drive us off. Then fall back to the church. If we can drive them away again, we can count on a long siege. I know Jake Tulley. He has the upper hand now and he won't give up. We'll have to hold out until help comes."

"H-how will we get any help?" Lady Priscilla gasped out as she shared the weight of a hamper of food with Christopher.

"That I haven't figured out yet. Remember this, though. We have to keep fighting. There's enough men out there to ride right over us."

SEVENTEEN

Jake Tulley sat slumped in his saddle. Somewhat over four hundred yards away, the cause of all his discomforts stood behind a wall and shot at his men. Anger reddened his face as he cursed Rebecca Caldwell and looked at the bodies lying in the strip of ground that separated them. A little puff of smoke appeared on the wall.

Smack! He had barely counted one when a slug splashed lead on a rock twenty feet away.

A Comanche lying near the rock let out a howl of pain and rolled away. He writhed on the ground for a moment, then sat up. Blood streamed from his eyes.

"Those gawddamned long-shootin' guns," Jake snarled so violently that Opie Dillon, beside him, cringed slightly.

"This ain't workin' too good," Opie observed.

"Yer damn right. Git that buck over here, the one Wild Horse left us for a messenger. We gotta make him understand he has to ride for Rolling Thunder's village and have the whole damned mess of warriors join us here. We gotta have more people than they have bullets or we'll never take that place."

"Right away, Boss."

Over the sights of his Jeffrey, Jason Plumm watched the gesticulating conversation between Jake Tulley and a squat, ugly Comanche. When the Indian turned his horse to ride away from the battle, Jason surmised his purpose. He took careful aim and squeezed off a round.

The heavy, 480 grain, paper-patched bullet took time reaching the target. With the brave riding away from Jason, the range became too great. Gravity proved the invisible victor once more and the slug struck the earth a good three feet behind the flying hoofs of the war pony.

"Bloody hell!" Jason cursed. "That devil is going for reinforcements. I'm certain of it."

"The problem is, where and how long it will take them to get here," Anthony Parrish observed.

"That's not a third of the number who attacked the rangers," Rebecca commented. "The Comanches must have a village close by. That's where he will go. By evening, or maybe in the morning, the whole band will be here."

"And then?" Sir Devon asked from his position at the gate below them.

"We'll definitely have to fort up in the chapel. We will be lucky not to have lost some people by that time," came Rebecca's grim reply.

*　　　*　　　*

Wild Horse chafed at the inactivity. This was not the way men fought. Where were the personal honors? Where the excitement of close armed conflict? The wall had weak places. They could ride into the compound. These were not tough, determined buffalo hunters caught in a good defensive position. There were women along and a child. Once inside, it would be easy.

Properly worked up by this line of thought, Wild Horse turned to his men and exhorted them to another charge. With shrill war whoops trembling on the air, they raced toward the mission.

Swiftly the distance narrowed. Then the long-speaking guns opened up from the walls. A brave shrieked in pain and toppled from his pony's back. Wild Horse yelled more encouragement and dashed ahead of his men. A horse buckled in the forelegs and crashed to the ground. Another warrior swerved to pick up his downed brother. Gradually the charge lost momentum. At a hundred-fifty yards, the volume of fire had grown too heavy. One by one, the Comanches turned away and raced for safety beyond range. At last only *Nis-ti-u-na* remained.

A valiant warrior, Wild Horse slowed his mount to a trot and swung back and forth over a short patch of ground, face turned toward the distant walls. He seemed oblivious of the lead that cracked through the air around him as he waved his war lance in defiance, shouted Comanche obscenities at the defenders, and then slowly, with utter contempt and rigid dignity, turned his pony and walked back to the perimeter.

After three hard-fought hours, the battle had become a stalemate. During a lull, Rebecca left the wall to refresh herself. She found Lady Priscilla sitting despondent among the few remnants of her possessions rescued from the inn. Pity touched the young girl and she settled beside the Britisher.

"Please believe me, Lady Priscilla. I am so sorry about your clothes. You had such beautiful things. I . . . I always admired them."

Priscilla looked at Rebecca as though seeing her for the first time. "I . . . why thank you. I'm afraid I have been rather unspeakably rude to you. After all, you did protect me from danger several times. Now we're all trapped here, and . . . and . . ." Tears filled her eyes. "And we're going to die. I should make amends."

"No apology needed," Rebecca offered magnanimously. "Don't be so certain that we will lose this fight. I know it's painful to you, with all you have lost, but the thing to do is not dwell on that, or our condition. What you should do is get mad. The Comanches, Jake Tulley's gang, the men out there, these are our enemy. Hate them for what they have done to us, what they did to you. Let yourself get good and angry at these filth. Then take up a rifle and join us in the fighting."

Priscilla blinked and her lips pursed with the effort of her concentration. "You know, you're right," she declared a moment later. "I'm not at all a bad shot, you know. I think . . . yes, why not. Give me a moment and then direct me to a spot. I must find my little Martini."

In less than five minutes, Lady Priscilla appeared with her Swiss-made Martini rifle. Rebecca directed her to one of the low portions of the wall, presently covered alone by Riggs.

"This collapsed section of wall is one of our weakest spots. If ever they get the idea they can come through here easily, we'll be fighting among the buildings. The more firepower we have here the less likely it is they will consider it."

A somewhat wild light in Lady Priscilla's eyes added

grim force to her words. "Then I shall be most happy to make it hot for them. Move over a bit, if you would, Riggs. There's some of the blighters coming our way now."

Lying stretched along the necks of their mounts, six of Wild Horse's warriors made a dash toward the breach in the wall. Visions of *coups* and many white scalps swam in their heads. Lady Priscilla coolly worked the underlever action of the single-shot Martini and inserted a 10.3x65 Baenziger cartridge. It resembled nothing so much as a brass casing for a .410 shotgun with a long slug of lead in the end. She closed the swing-down breech and took aim.

"Bit like popping a cape buffalo, don't you think?" she asked Riggs in a total abandonment of her usual haughty manner.

"Yes, Madam, quite a lot I'd say. Only these buggers think as well as move fast."

Eye back on her sights, Lady Priscilla adjusted her aim slightly, then set the sights for two hundred yards. The Martini spoke and a hostile went flying from his pony. She opened the breech and extracted the smoking casing. Quickly she reloaded.

"Good shooting, Lady Priscilla," Rebecca complimented.

"Oh, please, call me Priss."

Rebecca went back to her post somewhat stunned at this sudden about-face. Behind her, Riggs' double ten-gauge boomed and Priscilla's Martini cracked loudly.

Walt Cuttler, the leader of the Comanchero detachment, came to Jake Tulley in mid-afternoon. "Mister Tulley, you see them Comanch'? They got the right idea. Head for that breach. Only they're too few and they went about it wrong. We're doin' nothin' but sittin' here and stewin'. My boys don't like the delay.

"What I figger is, we could make it through there." He pointed again at the low spot in the wall. "I'll talk to ol' Wild Horse about his bucks ridin' close support for us and I think we can do it easy."

"I've sent for Rolling Thunder," Jake told him. "With some fifty more warriors, we can do it without any trouble. Me'n my boys ain't gonna move until we got more numbers. Go ahead and charge them if you want, though."

Cuttler reined his horse around and rode to where Wild Horse talked with the survivors of the last charge. Quickly he explained his idea and the war leader agreed. Cuttler rounded up his men and put spurs to his horse.

With Cuttler far in the lead, his Comancheros streaming out behind him, the Comanches screened to both sides, the strong contingent thundering over the the ground. They drew fire immediately, though ineffective. Closer they came until the five-foot adobe barricade loomed large in Cuttler's face. The Comanchero leader set spurs to his beast once more and it shot into the air.

It gracefully sailed over the broken wall and pile of rubble. Walt Cuttler opened his mouth to utter a frightening yell when a whiff of buckshot jerked him out of the saddle.

"Keep low, Madam," Riggs told Lady Priscilla. "They're going to try us again."

The lead man had grown so large in Riggs' sights that his figure blotted out everything else as his mount leaped over the crumbled wall. Riggs' trigger finger lightly fanned the thin metal tang, and a load of 00 buckshot spat from one ten-gauge barrel. Angry red spots, like giant pox marks, appeared on the rider's face and neck an instant before he disappeared from the sight picture. Quickly Riggs swung toward a second Comanchero who had crowded in close behind the first.

A bit too quickly, he discharged the second barrel. The shot column smashed into the side of the horse's head, nearly blowing it off the doomed animal. Its rider shot over the gory mess that had been its poll and right cheek and landed on his head. The dry-stick sound of his breaking neck told the valet that a follow-up round would not be necessary. All the same, Lady Priscilla already had him covered with her Martini.

Riggs opened the breech of his Drilling and began to insert fresh loads. As he did, the third Comanchero to approach the wall reined in short and swung his six-gun at Riggs' head.

Christopher Anderson had been pressed into service bringing ammunition to the defenders on the wall. Like everyone, he had been armed for his own protection. As he wrestled with a heavy wooden box of cartridges, he carried his light-weight Lancaster rifle over one shoulder, its sling biting into his flesh. When the first Comanchero came over the low wall, he dropped the box and grabbed for his weapon.

He no sooner fitted the butt-stock of the underlever single-shot .360 rifle to his shoulder than Riggs blew the intruder from his saddle. Riggs fired again by the time Christopher had checked his sights. Then the boy caught sight of the third man, aiming a revolver at Riggs' unsuspecting head.

The Lancaster slammed against Christopher's shoulder and the round plunked into the Comanchero's left ear. The 134 grain .360 No. 5 Rook bullet's 312 foot pounds of energy proved enough to pop the bandit's eyes from their sockets before he sagged to one side and slid off his horse.

For a moment, Christopher stood in stunned shock. "Oh, my God," he exclaimed haltingly. He forgot for the moment to clear his weapon and insert a fresh cartridge. Suddenly the scene swirled about him and his stomach churned like it had aboard *La Belle Marie* during the hurricane. Acid bile, and the remains of his hurriedly eaten breakfast, boiled up his throat and out past his lips. Bent double, the boy gagged and heaved until he had rid himself of the reaction to killing his first man. Suddenly Rebecca stood firmly beside him.

She placed an arm around his slender shoulders and squeezed the boy to her tender bosom. "Get ahold of yourself, Chris. I know it's rough the first time you kill someone. Don't let it upset you for long. The next one will be easier."

After the fiasco of the Comanchero attack, Jake Tulley fumed helplessly on a low knoll five hundred yards from the mission. He gathered Wild Horse and his braves and the surviving Comancheros.

"The day's draggin' on an' we're gettin' nowhere. We can't risk another attack until Rolling Thunder gets here with the rest of his warriors. What we've got here is a thing they call a siege. We have to surround that danged mission so's they can't get away. Everyone stay out of range of them big rifles, make yerselves seen, though, so they know there's no chance to break out. Spread out thin, but make sure you can see the fellers on both sides. We've gotta make the trap tight. Then, when Rolling Thunder gets here, we'll ride over that

180

damned Rebecca Caldwell 'n' her friends like a McCormick reaper eats wheat."

Darkness came with a lingering, colorful sunset, typical of the plains. From the wall, individual fires could be seen, indicating the ring of death that surrounded the mission. Rebecca studied them carefully before she met with Lone Wolf and Jason.

"They are too close to each other," she began. "There would be no chance for us all to ride out of here."

"One man could make it," Lone Wolf suggested. "We know what direction the rangers took. I could ride to them for help."

"Why not send one of our guides? Lord knows, they're knowledgeable about getting along on the prairie," Jason suggested.

Lone Wolf gave him a tolerant smile. "They are Delaware Indians. When it comes to people who have been fighting Indians for a long while, they are far more inclined to take the word of another white man than any Indian, 'civilized' or not. It's just the way things are in this country."

"My error, sorry," Jason relented. "You would be careful, though?"

"Bet on it. If I get caught, you would all die."

"Hurry, then," Rebecca urged him.

Lone Wolf waited another hour, then saddled his horse and padded its feet with burlap sacks to muffle the hoofbeats. He slipped quietly through a gap made by drawing the wagons part way back from the gate. Silently, on foot, he faded into the surrounding darkness.

Everyone waited tensely, expecting a shouted challenge and a fateful shot at any moment. Half an hour passed, then another, before Rebecca relaxed and felt certain Lone Wolf had evaded the ring of besiegers. She ate a hasty meal when Monson announced it served. Then she climbed to the parapet to relieve Cootyarkey so he could eat.

Jason found her there a few minutes later. Tenderly, silently he took her into his arms. They clung to each other with wordless desperation. Gently he kissed her lips, found them cold but eager to respond. A swelling began in his loins, though their danger quickly reduced his desire. They kissed again, transmitting what they found impossible to express. Jason's blunt fingers stroked one of her raven braids.

Rebecca's own desire sent shivers through her body. She knew the situation prevented any further intimacy, no matter how demanding her needs. When at last they stood a bit apart, her eyes filled momentarily with tears. Sunrise would decide their fate. A secret communication passed between them. In that instant, they both realized, only too well, that this might be the last night of their lives.

EIGHTEEN

Jake Tulley located Sonney Boyle in the thick blackness that precedes dawn. He hunkered down beside the young outlaw and they held a whispered conversation.

"I want you to gather some of the boys, say three, and take some of ol' Wild Horse's bucks. Anybody they got on watch oughta be purty droopy by now. You're to slip up on the wall and get over into the compound. We'll start a little attack, git their attention on the outside. Then you take to poppin' 'em off from inside the place. Got it?"

"You sure this will work?"

"I been thinkin' on it off an' on all night. Supposin' ol' Rolling Thunder decides he don't want any part o' this turkey shoot. In that case, this way's our only chance."

"If you say so, Boss. I'll git started right now."

It took fifteen minutes for Sonney to gather his forces. He gave them a whispered briefing and they began to crawl toward the silent mission.

Sonney used the period of darkness wisely. They angled across the front of the high wall and around on one side. There he had earlier observed another eroded section. He signaled his men by touch to remain quiet while he made sure no sentries lurked nearby. When he became satisfied that they remained undetected, Sonney led them over the broken adobe blocks and into the grounds of the mission. The group paused in deep shadow while Sonney studied the terrain.

"The best place would be the belfry of that church. We can shoot down on 'em all around from there."

"How we gonna get there?" one of the gang asked.

"Why don't you just walk up, go through the door an' climb the ladder?" Sonney returned sarcastically. "With that place they was stayin' burned down, chances are the whole bunch will be sleepin' in the church. Now that room off to the side ain't got a roof, so they wouldn't figger it to be safe. Block it off from the rest of the inside, most likely.

"What we gotta do is get in there, climb up to the rafters, and make it the rest of the way on the outside of the steeple."

"That sounds dangerous to me," another gunslick remarked.

"Not all that much. Most of the plaster is gone and there are large cracks that offer pretty good holds. One of us can scale it, then drop down a rope for the others to use."

"Who's that one gonna be, Sonney?"

"No reason it shouldn't be me. We'll go across that open space two at a time. Ready?"

A pale band of white announced false dawn by the time the invaders reached the rafters of the damaged vestry. Sonney and three more of Tulley's gunhawks hurried along the ridge pole like so many circus artists and hugged the side of the bell tower. Sonney pulled off his boots, flexed his toes and started hunting footholds.

"Gimme that rope you got," he told the man next to him. With the coils looped over his head, he started to climb. Part way up, his foot slipped on some grainy pebbles of adobe and Sonney hung precariously until he could find a secure place to rest his weight. He dug his head into his shoulder to wipe away sweat that beaded on his forehead, then resumed his climb.

Panting, every muscle in his arms and legs aching from the exertion, Sonney slowly closed on the open arch, through which the clapper, lip, and leader of the bell could be seen. He pulled himself higher and threw an arm over the stool of the opening. He hung there a second, panting, while the dimly seen ground beyond the wall seemed to swim in his vision. Then he swung his body sideways and hauled with all his might. With a little wriggling, he made his way inside.

Sonney lay back against the cool adobe and fought his breath back to normal. Then he secured the loose end of the rope to the upright of the ladder and dropped the coil outside. Within seconds, the first man's head cleared the arch. Two more came up quickly. The remainder would have already found advantageous places in the vestry.

"All right, boys, pick yourselves a place and we wait for Jake to attack."

Linc Mitchell chose to cover the area at the front of the church. He settled down and rested his Winchester on the adobe blocks that formed the arch. To his left, Karl Mueller faced to the south. Sonney covered the west and Pearly Nabb had the north. Brightness grew steadily in the east.

Lady Priscilla came from the church, a small iron

pot of oatmeal in one hand, a granite pot of coffee in the other. She started toward the gate where Issac and her husband stood watch. Halfway there she paused and glanced back to see if Christopher followed her with the rest of breakfast. Indistinct movement caused her to look upward. She saw a man silhouetted in the belfry.

"I say, who's that up there? You'll have to climb down for breakfast, I'm afraid. I'm terrified of heights." When she received no answer, she tried again. "Hullo. Is that you, Sir Devon?"

The crack of a Winchester answered her.

The slug smashed its way through the coffee pot, deflected upward and went into the fleshy part of her right arm. Priscilla screamed as scalding coffee splashed over her hand. The metal container was ripped from her grasp and went flying. As she sank to the ground, a roar of anger came from her husband.

At the gate, Anthony Parrish whirled around at the sound of the shot and saw his wife fall. He looked upward, his rifle already headed for his shoulder. Instantly he spotted the man with the Winchester. One hammer of his Rigby came back and dropped on the firing pin.

A 480 grain Rigby Match bullet sped toward the bell tower, propelled by eighty-five grains of black powder. At that short range, it struck with a muzzle energy of slightly less than eighteen hundred foot pounds. The impact flattened the slug as it powdered a worn, ancient adobe block which provided little hindrance before it hit Linc Mitchell square in the chest.

The gunhawk jerked backward and his head struck the bell. A solemn bong sounded the departure of his soul while his body plummeted down through the opening toward the floor of the narthex.

Immediately, Anthony fired the second barrel,

which sent a bullet ploughing lengthwise through Karl Mueller's shoulders. The wounded gunman screamed in agony and tried to turn toward his attacker.

"You idiot!" Sonney shrieked down the tower opening. In the next second, two more guns opened up on his carefully selected ambush site.

Flying slugs made a bedlam of sound when they contacted the waist and hip of the bell. Hideous vibrations assaulted the ears of the men trapped in the belfry. The survivors hunkered below the open arches and held hands to their ears. Except for Karl Mueller who could not move his arms upward. He sheltered from the flurry of lead in the best manner he could and screamed in agony at the punishment his head took from the incessant clangor. When he could stand it no longer, he stood upright and fired wildly at his oppressors.

Two slugs ripped into his belly and he sprawled over the stool of the arch. A thick trickle of red ran down, staining the brown adobe as it soaked into the weathered surface. The firing slackened.

Pearly Nabb hazarded a quick peek over the rounded blocks in front of him.

Instantly his forehead came into the field of Anthony's sights. The Farquharson bellowed again. The .450 Rigby bullet made a large, bruise-circled hole between and an inch above Pearly's eyes, mushed his brain and blew out a large chunk of his skull. A crimson shower splattered on Sonney Boyle.

"I got them. I got the bloody bastards!" Anthony shouted. He ran to his wife and lifted her gently into his arms.

"Priss . . . Priss. Are you all right?"

"I-it hurts awfully. And I'm a bit swimmy in the head."

"Can you walk?"

"I think so."

"Let me help you. Effie and Basil can dress your wound."

"I burned my hand, too, I'm afraid," Lady Priscilla said in a faraway voice. "Does it mean I won't be able to shoot for a while?"

"No, my pet. Provided you can do it left-handed."

Man and wife walked to the door of the church and entered. Only then did the realization strike Anthony that they would have to cross under the opening to the belfry. What if there had been more of them up there? And how the bloody hell had they gotten there in the first place? He saw the spread-eagled corpse oozing blood on the tile floor of the narthex and skirted it hurriedly, nearly dragging Priscilla along.

"Tend to her, will you, please?" he commanded Effie when the maid came forward. Immediately the girl broke into tears. "Enough of that, Effie. See to your mistress."

"Yes, yer Lordship," she sniffled.

Anthony turned to go when he saw a strange tableau.

Rebecca stood with her back tightly against the wall near the ladder to the bell tower. She shook her head in a negative gesture and waggled a finger from side to side, then pointed upward. Anthony took it rightly to mean he should stand still, that another of the swine waited above.

Swiftly, the remarkable beauty, her face distorted in a mask of silent fury, went up the ladder two rungs at a time. Near the top she drew her .44 American and showed it ahead of her. Her shoulders disappeared beyond the flooring of the belfry, and she came to an abrupt halt. Anthony heard her words, distorted slightly by the inner curve of the bell, as a disembodied voice from the heavens.

"Hello, Sonney. You remember me, don't you?

Rebecca Caldwell."

Sonney Boyle stared fixedly into the black hole in the Smith and Wesson. His own weapon forgotten, the big .44 held the same fascination that a cobra did for a small furry creature. He blinked his eyes once and nodded slightly. He tried to swallow the lump in his throat and it only stuck harder, a cactus pear of terror lodged by its spines.

"This is for my mother and for me."

Rebecca's .44 exploded in the stillness.

She paused a moment, then began to descend the rungs of the ladder.

By ten o'clock, Jake Tulley had begun to worry. No sign of Rolling Thunder. The way he figured it, the water and ammunition must be running low for the defenders. He had called off the planned dawn attack when something went wrong and shots exploded from inside the compound. He felt certain there would be no survivors. Reason said that another final sweep would wipe out Rebecca Caldwell and the rest. He would give it another hour and see what happened then.

At ten-forty, the messenger returned. "*Kansaleumko*, warriors go Palo Duro Canyon," he said in bad English.

"Why? Why did they do that?"

"*Chemakacho* send them."

"Damn Roger Styles and his ambition!" he railed aloud. "He's left us cut off here." Jake looked around, desperate for a plan. Slowly a wicked grin began to spread.

"Let's say," he told Opie Dillon, "that I'm right. They ain't got much water, low on ammunition, maybe short of food. Some of 'em could have been wounded, or killed. They got one chance and one only. If we pull out."

"We gonna do that?" Opie asked, slowly blinking his eyes.

"No, damnit! Hell, no. An' we ain't gonna sit around here and starve 'em out either. One big attack. Everybody we got left. From all directions at once. We move in, get over them walls and butcher 'em like sheep in a slaughter house. Git everyone ready, Opie."

Opie came back ten minutes later. "Hoss Jenkins has got some dynamite."

Jake rubbed his hands together gleefully. "Good. Good. We'll use that, too. They'll think a whole damned army is after 'em." The idea appealed. Jake assumed a military pose. "My compliments to Mister Jenkins and will he divide up his dynamite as well as his Comancheros so that we can strike from four sides at once?"

The renegade horde rode from every direction, charging down on the defenses with wild yells and shrill war whoops. Jason had been loading ammunition in an attempt to recover their expenditures from the previous day. When the alarm sounded, he set aside the Newton straight line reloading tool and hurried to the wall.

"You'll have to fight, too, Basil," he ordered over his shoulder.

"Me, sir? Oh, my heavens, m'Lord. I've never touched a firearm."

"You'll learn, or die."

Bullets whined overhead and others thudded heavily into the adobe walls. From the parapet, Rebecca observed Comanche warriors racing ahead, armed with oddly misshapen arrows. Thin wisps of smoke curled from under the shafts, where bulky cylinders had been attached. The charging braves ignored an increasing fusilade of slugs that split the air near to them. At less than twenty-five yards, they released their projectiles.

The strange arrows flew over the walls and two landed on the roof of the monastic cells. A second later they exploded with a tremendous roar.

Dynamite, Rebecca thought with a sinking heart. Six more of the deadly missiles went off, punishing the defenders' ears. One obliterated the roofed-over well casing, which sent a shower of stone chips flying. Rebecca felt a sting on her cheek and the warm trail of blood. A sharp pain came in her right thigh when a flat piece of rock slapped against her. She'd carry a bad bruise, she thought. Off to her left, poor Basil clumsily loaded a Purdy shotgun and swung the barrels over the wall.

When he fired the first barrel, it staggered him backward. He touched the second off into the fury-twisted face of a screaming hostile who clawed at the inner surfaces of a Vee-shaped breach near the top of the wall. Before the wine steward could open the Parker to reload, another howling savage crawled over the side, ignoring the deep cuts in his thighs. He jerked back his tomahawk and let it fly, handle rotating over blade in a smooth arc until it landed in its target.

Keen steel cleaved into Basil's forehead and he dropped without even a sigh. The Purdy clattered on the walkway.

Immediately Rebecca blew the Comanche back over the wall with two shots from the Smith and Wesson .44 American.

"Goddamn him to bloody hell!" Christopher shouted. He took quick aim and put a .360 bullet into the throat of another Comanche. "Basil wasn't a bad fellow, actually." Tears filled the boy's eyes, but he quickly reloaded. "He didn't do nasty things. It was all a joke between us." He brought up the Lancaster and sighted on a grinning Comanchero who had leaped the five-foot breach further along the wall and aimed at Rebecca's back.

A grunt of surprise and disbelief burst from the renegade's chest when the No. 5 Rook slug slapped into his rigid belly. A purple-gray loop of intestine protruded and he gazed wonderingly at it while Lady Priscilla, awkward in her left-handed stance, finished him with a load of buckshot in his gaping mouth.

"There's a good lad," she shouted to Christopher. "Get another one for me."

Suddenly the volume of fire from outside tripled in intensity. "To the church. They're coming over the walls," Jason yelled above the cacophony of battle. "Fight your way to the church."

"No. Wait!" Rebecca commanded. "Stand fast, everyone. It's Lone Wolf and the rangers."

An instant later, shots blasted toward her from the damaged vestry.

"Over there, me hearties!" Riggs shouted, a finger pointed at the source of sniper fire. Three heavy sporting rifles opened up on the hidden outlaws.

Rebecca felt a tug at her sleeve and a hot, stinging sensation in her left arm. A bullet had creased her, she knew. Both of her revolvers had been emptied and she put them aside to pick up the shotgun dropped by Basil. She found seven brass shells in the top pocket of his leather soumelier's apron. Quickly she reloaded and sent a gibbering black Comanchero off to the celestial watermelon patch with a load of buckshot. Below her she saw Lord Anthony running toward the vestry.

Clutched in one hand he held one of the explosive

arrows that had a defective fuse. In the other he carried a match. A burst of fire tried to find him, and he ducked behind the curved outer wall at the rear of the altar dome, struck the match and lighted the short length of black fuse. When it sputtered to life he popped out and hurled it through a shattered window of the vestry.

When the blast came, it raised ancient dust, charred rafters, pieces of Comanches, and Jake Tulley's hidden outlaws. Rebecca turned her attention to the plain outside the compound.

Comanche warriors, a few straggling Comancheros, and the bulk of Jake Tulley's gang raced away across the brown prairie. The rangers streamed after them, six-guns blazing.

A sudden quiet fell over the compound.

Captain Slone put a silver whistle to his lips and a shrill summons went out to recall the pursuing Texans. "Assemble on me!" the ranger officer commanded.

In fifteen minutes, order had been restored and the wounded had all been treated. Captain Slone met with Rebecca, Lone Wolf, and Jason.

"We cut sign that indicates the main body of the Comanches are headed toward Palo Duro Canyon. Odds are the survivors of this outfit will join up with them."

"We're going with you," Rebecca declared. "I'll not rest until I catch Jake Tulley and finish him."

"You've had a rough time of it, Miss Caldwell. A night's rest would surely be in order."

"Like you said," Lone Wolf put in, "your friend Colonel Goodnight will have a rough time of it. We want to be along. If we ride all night, when can we reach Palo Duro?"

"Some time tomorrow. But . . ."

"We can manage."

"Come now. We're all drawn thin," Sir Devon protested. "A day's rest is what we need. I see no reason to go haring off after these savages. Besides, Jason, you have your position to consider."

"There are people in trouble. We are going to help them," Jason told him icily.

"I agree. I can be ready in half an hour," Anthony Parrish declared.

"My husband is right. We must do what we can," Lady Priscilla said forcefully. She turned a warm smile and kindly eyes on Rebecca. "You should rest . . . but this is important."

"Bully good!" Riggs roared. "Then it's all decided? We ride for this Palo, ah, whatever it is, Canyon."

NINETEEN

It had come at them suddenly, Jake Tulley recalled. His men and the Comancheros had reached the main contingent of Rolling Thunder's band in mid-afternoon. They rode together across a vast, gently rolling plateau that seemed to stretch, uninterrupted, to the ends of the earth. The large band of raiders had covered several miles when suddenly a vast cleft in the ground opened before them.

Sheer, red-tinted walls dropped from the plain around to the thin, glistening ribbon of a river below, made tiny by the distance. The mighty canyon twisted in the tortured, sinuous patterns of an ancient and powerful water course.

"Down there," Rolling Thunder told him, "is your enemy, Goodnight. We must strike fast, for the one called Goodnight has friends among the people of Quanah Parker. He is chief over the Quahadi Comanche."

"Goodnight got cattle down there?" Jake asked.

"No," a Comanchero replied. "They are coming down from Colorado. A month, maybe more, the herds will be here."

"Damn. I was figgerin' that iffin we could stampede them through those narrows, there'd be a chance we could smash Goodnight and his cowboys flat with little risk to us."

"There are some buildings, a house being built. There is a possibility that Goodnight will not even be here. He comes and goes, keeping touch with his cattle on the trail."

"Whatever's down there ain't gonna be after we get through," Jake growled.

It took more than an hour to get to the floor of the canyon. Not an over sensitive man, Jake shared the feelings of awe and menace that infected the other men. Palo Duro Canyon *was* impressive. The combined force made an early camp and sent scouts forward to look over the situation at the ranch.

Work went on around the small stone house being constructed as the ranch headquarters. A barn had been nearly completed, lacking only the siding on the second story. A well had been dug, Opie Dillon reported to Jake. A pump house had been completed around it and the scaffolding of a windmill partially erected above this. The cowboys had also built a large wooden storage tank to hold water, fed by gravity to the corrals, bunkhouse, and unfinished stone dwelling. A tidy, prosperous-looking place. Jake and Roger Styles met with Rolling Thunder and his subordinates and Jenkins of the Comancheros.

"We can move in during the night and hit 'em at dawn," Jake suggested. The other leaders nodded in agreement. "You have any more of that dynamite, Jenkins?"

"Yep. Only I wouldn't want to be usin' it with them

big ol' cliffs hangin' over our heads. Might set off a rock slide that would bury us along with Goodnight an' his crew."

They settled on a plan, whereby Rolling Thunder's Comanches would attack first, followed by the rest in a second wave.

Jake smiled with satisfaction as the second line swept down on the Goodnight ranch. The Comanches had swarmed in, shouting and shooting. Two hands had gone down before they could reach for their weapons. The rest took shelter in and among the partially constructed buildings. Rolling Thunder's men had rolled through the ranchyard with ease. Before the stunned cowboys could recover, Jake led the next charge.

Firing to left and right, Jake guided his mount with his knees and howled gleefully as the outlaw horde thundered down on the widely spaced buildings. A head appeared in a barn window and Jake thumbed off a shot.

The man gave a short, shrill cry and spun away, face riddled with wood splinters from the slug that had struck the sill an inch below his face, punched through and put a hole in his chest. Elated, Jake rode on.

In a flash they passed through the clearing. On the far side, the Comanches had already turned around and prepared to make another dash through the defenders' poorly chosen positions.

Then the unexpected happened.

Rather than having been cowed by the surprise attack, the cowboys had simply taken cover in cellars and ditches while the storm rolled over them. Now they rose up and began to pump fire into the backs of

Tulley's men and the faces of the charging Comanches. Shots came, too, Jake saw, from small caves in the canyon wall behind the place, across the swirling waters of a small creek.

"At 'em, boys!" Jake shouted and the conglomeration of white rabble charged again.

It seemed to Jake that he had only blinked his eye. In that brief time, more riders appeared. They swung out of the trees in a wide arc and attacked Rolling Thunder's warriors. Jake took a shot at a careless cowboy whose head popped around the corner of the barn, then ducked as a shotgun boomed not far away. Then they were through the yard and closing on Rolling Thunder's men. Jake shook his head in disbelief.

It looked as though Comanches fought Comanches. The two lines of Indians clashed with each other then swept apart. The next instant, Jake found himself face to face with a screaming Comanche. Unlike the red war paint of Rolling Thunder's band, these warriors wore dabs and bars of black. The brave thrust with a war lance, which Jake parried with his revolver barrel. The horses collided, front shoulder to shoulder. With his left hand, Jake drew a long, wicked-bladed knife and drove it into the Comanche's taut abdomen.

His war cry cut off in mid-bark and the warrior's face went pale. Jake twisted and jerked his knife free. Confident of his kill, he turned aside to find another target, only to realize that they were outnumbered.

"Pull back," he shouted. "Fall back on our Comanches."

In moments, the attack broke off. Jake sought Rolling Thunder.

"What the hell's goin' on?" he demanded.

"Quahadi Comanche," Rolling Thunder explained.

198

"They come, help Goodnight. Quanah send them. We no fight."

"What do you mean you won't fight?" Jake growled angrily .

"They are brothers. No fight. We go now."

"Like hell you do. You stand your goddamned ground."

At his side, Roger raised a placating hand. "Do you mean you won't fight the whites either?"

"No fight anyone. We attack Goodnight, Quahadis fight us."

"So," Roger summarized. "You won't fight the Quahadis and you won't fight Goodnight. Will you at least stay here and protect our flank?"

"No fight," Rolling Thunder repeated with inflexible determination.

When Rolling Thunder's braves raced down on the ranch, Charles Goodnight himself, saw them first. "Suck up yer balls, boys. We're in for a heller!" he shouted as he reached for a Spencer rifle resting in the doorway of the barn.

He coolly shot at the swarming savages as they dashed through the ranchyard. Then came the second wave of whites.

"I'll be a son of a bitch! Those are white renegades," the ruggedly handsome man declared. Already approaching middle age, the broad-shouldered Goodnight had not a streak of gray in his hair. His face was that of a man ten years younger and it nobly supported a clean, straight nose and a flourishing mustache. He calmly blew a Comanchero out of his saddle and squatted below the wall of the barn.

"Back in yer holes, fellers, they're comin' again," Goodnight shouted when the Comanches charged once more.

When both waves had flashed past the buildings, Goodnight assessed the situation as somewhat grim. Then he brightened as a large force of riders appeared around the bend and streamed out of a stand of trees.

"I'll be dipped in skunk shit!" he hollered. "Quanah has sent some of his braves to lend a hand. Get up, boys. Get up and give 'em hell out there."

Goodnight and his cowboys continued to fire at the enemy while the two Comanche bands clashed and disengaged. Goodnight's shrewd mind had no difficulty determining what went on when the Quahadis crossed a small stream and lined out in fighting formation, while the hostiles did the same along a low ridge carved by the mighty river eons ago. Without saying a word, Goodnight realized, the brother Comanches had accepted a standoff. That would let him and his boys take care of those renegades.

A long minute passed in silence on both sides, then the scruffy-dressed outlaws attacked again.

With Rolling Thunder neutralized, Roger Styles thought angrily, the attack had gone badly from the start. He had ordered his men to get in among the buildings, dismount and carry the fight to the cowboys on foot. Now he had been pinned down by withering fire, crouched behind the pump house, the windmill tower and storage tank looming over him. Bullets from friend and foe turned the air around him into a hornet's nest of cracks and buzzes. To his left a Comanchero rose to get a better field of fire, only to start to gag and gurgle on a fountain of blood that spurted from the hole in his throat. Next to the dying man, another of Jenkins' men fired a shot and jumped to the right.

In mid-stride, he staggered and went down, both hands clutching a wound in his thigh, from which a steady stream of crimson stained a gory circle on his trouser leg. Roger heard a clatter and looked behind him to see another Comanchero start up the wooden strips that formed a ladder for the windmill.

A third of the way to the top, the man let out a weak cry and his arms flew off the tread above him as he swayed, then toppled away with a brief scream that ended when he broke his back over an exposed rafter of a small stone cooling house behind him. Roger faced front to return fire.

One of Jake Tulley's men made a run for the partly built barn. Roger heard the reports and watched in shock as the outlaw took hits from four directions at once. Shot to doll rags, he jerked and staggered, then fell into a twitching heap. Roger looked away to a more grim view.

Off to his right, to the south, across the shallow creek that fed into the Red River, sat the Quahadi Comanches. Weapons at the ready, they remained unmoving, arms crossed over chests. A small enough force to be taken, Roger reasoned, but sufficient to compel a stalemate with Rolling Thunder's band. No accounting for Injuns, though, he reminded himself. So long as they stayed on the field, they constituted a deadly threat to his men.

"Ignorant savage brute," Roger cursed Rolling Thunder aloud. "He said he wanted to fight. So why doesn't he do so?"

The volume of fire increased from the defenders. Roger emptied the magazine of his Winchester and drew a revolver from under his coat. "Pour it on, boys!" he shouted to the men. "Give 'em all you got so

201

we can get back out of here."

"Couple of miles is all," Captain Alan Slone told Rebecca and Jason. "Hear the shootin'?"

In the distance, the rattle of gunfire echoed clearly off the high walls of Palo Duro Canyon. Slone had led the rangers and his volunteers into the canyon not far from where Rolling Thunder made his descent. Now they raced against time toward the small clearing that Charles Goodnight had staked out as his new ranch headquarters.

"That's a lot of fire," Jason observed.

"Figger maybe seventy Comanches, plus the whites who got away at the mission. Goodnight can't have more than ten hands working there at this time. Could be we're already too late."

Rolling Thunder eased himself in his stirrupless saddle and glowered across the space that separated him from his Quahadi brothers. His anger was great and in his heart he felt betrayed. What had come to pass that Comanche fought Comanche? That both battled on the side of white men? What choices did he have?

He could ride out with his men. Yet, that would be seen as a sign of weakness by whites and the Quahadi alike. He could forget the bonds of brotherhood and attack Goodnight. That would in turn bring the Quahadis down on his band. Perhaps he should send a messenger to the war chief appointed by Quanah and suggest that they join forces, wipe out the *Chemakacho* and his men, then sweep over Goodnight and his cowboys. Wipe the whole country clean of whites. No. Quanah Parker and Goodnight had become brothers. If he, *Kansaleumko*, did this then Quanah would make war with his band until the last woman and child had been taken captive and the warriors' bones bleached in the sun. In an instant, Rolling Thunder's options changed rapidly.

One of his trail guards came dashing toward him, shouting that more whites approached the battle. A hundred yards behind him, a large force galloped through the sparse stands of trees and shallow pools at the bottom of the canyon.

A second later they opened fire on his warriors. Rolling Thunder immediately recognized the big man, standing in his stirrups at the lead. It was Slone of the rangers.

"Pull back. *Osolo*, organize a rear guard. Hold the rangers while we leave this place."

Jake Tulley wore the expression of a man who bore all the burdens of the world. He blinked in disbelief as Rolling Thunder signaled his braves to ride off. Only a few remained, under command of Big Wolf, to fire at a line of riders who hurtled down on the small rear guard. God, he realized with a start, it was the rangers. He hurried over to where Roger strained to swing into the saddle.

"What can we do now? Rolling Thunder's run off. We've got Goodnight's cowboys in front of us, them damned Quahadi Comanches blockin' off our escape to the south. Now we got the damned rangers at our backs."

"We have to make a run for it. North, across the river and along that cliff face."

203

"They'll pick us off like flies."

"What do you think will happen if we stay here?"

There seemed to be no battle at all. Only a few Comanches firing at the rangers and some shots coming from in among the buildings ahead. Rebecca sat her saddle, anxious to come to grips with Tulley. Beside her, she heard Captain Slone issue crisp orders.

"Five of you men stay here. The rest come on, after those Comanches. We'll drive 'em out of the canyon and back to the south."

A nearly continuous roar rose as the rangers charged the rear guard. Big Wolf and all his braves died in a matter of seconds and the Texans rode over them, hot in pursuit of Rolling Thunder. Rebecca looked around and saw movement among the ranch structures.

"Down there," she called out. "That looks like Jake Tulley. The gang is getting away." She drew a heavy .44 and urged Ike into a fast trot.

Lone Wolf and Jason hurried after her.

Bullets cracked through the air around Opie Dillon as he ran with the others toward the Red River. One slug tugged at the cloth of his shirt sleeve and added another burst of speed. Suddenly he found himself knee-deep in swirling water. Many of his friends had already struck out to swim to the other side. Opie turned back toward the advancing cowboys and the swarm of people on horseback who charged in their direction. Indecision and fear tugged at him and he whimpered without knowing it.

"What's the matter?" Jake Tulley demanded as he

roughly grabbed Opie's shoulder.

"I . . . I can't swim, Jake. Oh, God, am I scared of water."

"You figger to stay here and take a bullet?"

Opie's eyes widened, showing a lot of white. "Oh, dearie me, no. But, honest, I don't know how to get across. Ain't there some boats?"

"No such luck," Jake told him. "You stay against this bank and keep them cowboys' heads down. I'll find someone who will help you across."

"Don't leave me, Jake. I'll drown if I have to try it alone," Opie begged.

Jake sloshed off through the water. A moment later, Opie heard him speaking to another outlaw. "Sammy, get over there an' help Opie. He can't swim."

"Sure, Boss," Sammy replied. "I done took me two boys over. One more won't hurt none."

Opie trembled with relief. He raised up and put a slug in the leg of a cowboy who leaped a corral rail and ran toward the river. A howl of pain came from his victim, who tumbled in the dust.

Then Sammy stood panting beside him. "Nothin' to it, Opie. Jist put up your iron, take a deep breath and hold yer head up high. Ever' time I tell you, let out your breath and take another. Now, lay out fell length in the water."

"I . . . I'll drown."

"Hush up, damnit. You do as I say and it'll be all right. Stretch out, stretch out an' hold yer head high. That's it."

Sammy eased into the water and took Opie by the collar. With a strong, sure stroke he struck out for the distant bank. Behind them horses thundered up to the near shore.

"There. In the water," a woman's voice called out. "Get those two."

Small spouts of water rose around Sammy and Opie, accompanied by wet chugs as the slugs bit into the surface. In nearly the same instant, they heard the reports of several weapons. Opie risked his stability to take a quick look over his shoulder.

"Oh, my God," he nearly wept with fear and frustration. "It's that Rebecca Caldwell. Hurry, Sammy. Don't let her get me."

"All right, boys. Gather around," Charles Goodnight called to his hands. "Round up your mounts and get your gear aboard. We're goin' after them damned Comanches with the rangers. Quanah calls Rolling Thunder and his band renegades, but I call 'em plain, ever'day sons of bitches. These here folks can deal with that white scum."

On the far bank of the Red, Jake Tulley watched Sammy safely arrive with Opie Dillon. Then he turned and hurried off to the north. Large boulders and runnels of loose stones blocked his way. He fell once and staggered on, the palm of his left hand dripping blood from a nasty gash. All around him, the remnants of his gang and the last five Comancheros struggled to put distance between them and the vengeful guns across the river. He heard loud shouts and heavy splashes.

"Gawdamn, they're swimming their hosses across," Toby Waters exclaimed.

"We don't have much chance against that," Jake reasoned aloud. "They can ride us down easy." His eyes searched for some means of escape.

A bit further along, he saw dark shadows in a rock face that should have been bright with sunlight. Caves, he realized as he tripped over another head-sized boulder and went sprawling in the debris of fossils, rocks, and sand. He came gasping to his feet.

"Roger!" he shouted. "Up there. Look at them caves. We can make a stand there."

Roger Styles came to Jake's side. His fancy clothing had become stained, rumpled, and torn. He had lost his low-crown beaver hat in the crossing. "I'm about winded. Is it right that the Caldwell girl and her followers are swimming their horses across?"

"Only too true," Jake informed him. His hand stung, as did both knees, and sweat ran into his eyes. "We gotta fight somewhere, it might as well be in those caves."

"I think you're right, Jake. You take the men on up and post them. When I reach there, I'll do a little exploring."

In five minutes, Jake had his men in position. Roger and a wounded outlaw staggered in together. Then the once dapper master criminal selected one man to accompany him. The young outlaw fashioned a torch from a bone-dry stick, which he frayed on one end with his Bowie knife.

"We'll be back, after we have a look around," Roger promised.

While the cornered bandits waited for their pursuers, Jake had his own inspection. Ignorant of the world's past, he had no appreciation for the evidence of cataclysmic changes that had gone on in this region over a period of ninety million years. The thick bands of differing stone, layers of fossils, and compressed, petrified vegetable matter held no meaning to him.

At least four different geological ages lay exposed to Jake's eyes. What did strike his untutored brain with superstitious dread were the pictographs, obviously painted by men long dead, that depicted strange and hideous monsters with the bodies of reptiles and great, gnashing teeth, of huge, woolly creatures with trunks and long tusks. Deeply shaken, he returned to his men to find their enemy had moved into range.

"They're up in those caves," Rebecca said, pointing.

"All these caves are considered sacred by the Comanche. They use them for ceremonies that go back before even the Spanish came here," one of the rangers told her.

"That's why the Quahadi didn't join us?"

"Yes, Miss Caldwell. They're not too happy about us comin' here, an' if any of these renegades get out, the Quahadi will make sure they take a long time dyin'."

Shots crackled from the caves above.

TWENTY

Bullets richocheted off the inner walls, moaning like lost souls, as Roger Styles worked his way back toward the bright circle that opened onto day. Jake had, he saw, positioned the men well, and they had engaged the attacking force at enough distance to deny them good targets. He summoned Tulley with a gesture, and they stepped to the back of the outer chamber, away from the ears of the other outlaws.

"I've found a way out. There are three chambers like this," he began and Jake interrupted.

"Yeah. I've been in the next one. Kinda scary. What's them strange animals painted on the walls? An' who done it?"

"Never mind that. The important thing is we can get out. Beyond the third room there are some low branches that go off in several directions. Perhaps an underground river system at one time. My point is that one of those leads to another cave, low down near the water. It comes out around that next bend, a good ways from where the boys have the Caldwell girl and her friends pinned down."

Jake brightened. "I'll tell the boys an' we can start fixin' torches, then we can make a run for it."

"Don't get ahead of yourself," Roger cautioned, one hand on Jake's arm to restrain him. "Think it over. We can't all go. That should be obvious."

Enlightenment came slowly. "Ye-ah. Iffin we do, that bunch out there will get wise and be on our trail in no time."

"That's right, Jake. We have to leave enough men behind to make them think we are all in here. They figure that we're trapped. All they have to do is hold on and starve us out. Only we know better now. Those Comancheros with Jenkins mean nothing to us. We can leave them behind as a rear guard."

"Yeah."

"Pick only our best men. Good gunhands, fellows who can think for themselves. The rest can stay."

Jake gave Roger a hard look, then dismissed the lives of those he would cull out with all the indifference his partner had shown. "I can put Opie Dillon in charge. He's almost as bad about li'l girls as that damned Bobby O'Toole. An' he's dumb, oh, is he dumb."

"Is he stupid enough to stay here and fight to the last man?" Roger asked eagerly.

"Yep. You can count on that."

"Good," the former banker purred. "Set it up. We have to be moving before those people out there decide to take more effective action."

"They ain't doin' nothin' out there but keepin' their heads down," Opie told Jake a minute later. "Did the big boss find a way out?"

"He did," Jake told him calmly. Then he took a casual breath and slipped in the lie. "It's a long way an' it's dark. I'm givin' you an important job. I want you

210

take charge here while we set up a chain o' the fellers to guide everyone out. You gotta hold that bunch until we pass the word to come on. Then hurry like hell and we all get outta here free as birds."

"That's a fine plan, Jake. I gotta hand it to ya. I'll do you good, Jake. You can count on me."

Jake put a hand on Opie's shoulder and gripped him tightly. "I know you will, Opie. That's why I picked you."

Five minutes later, amid a fusillade from the rear guard, the picked survivors quickly worked their way through the caves toward escape.

Tulley's men had all the advantages, Rebecca observed. They held the high ground and had excellent cover inside the cave. Anyone who tried to move directly up slope came under devastating fire. The thing to do, she decided, would be to get beyond them, where they could not see what happened, then climb up to a level with the opening, or slightly above. She went to her horse, Jason a step behind her.

"What are you going to do?"

"Get around there where they can't see me. Then climb up and fire into the cave."

"Good idea. I'm coming along."

"You . . . all right, Jason. Get your mount."

When fire slackened from the cave, the determined pair spurred their horses and rode further up the bank of the Red. The moment the mouth of the cave disappeared from view, Rebecca called a halt.

"Here's where we climb," she decided.

Progress was difficult. Nearly vertical walls challenged them. Rebecca wore moccasins, which made her ascent considerably easier. She found hand and toe holds and began to scale the cliff at a slow, though steady pace. Jason had left his cumbersome Jeffrey behind, accepting Rebecca's pistol belt and one of the Smith and Wesson .44s. His hard leather-soled, English boots labored at taking purchase, and he frequently slipped, throwing his weight on his hands and arms.

Fossilized shellfish and creatures of ages past, embedded in the porous stone and earth of the cliff, quickly shredded the skin off his fingers. He bit his lip at each new slash and maintained silence as he struggled upward. Ahead of him, Rebecca reached a narrow ledge that slanted up and back toward the cave. She started off along it, two hundred feet above the canyon floor, and heard Jason's gasp of relief when he reached the easier going.

Abruptly, the ledge ended. Once more, Rebecca started to climb, taking time for a quick glance back at Jason. She kept her eyes on another shelf that slanted around the bend, which her memory told her continued at an upward angle to a spot directly beside the cave. This must be the path, she speculated, used by Comanche medicine men to reach their sacred chambers. Behind her she heard a violent scrabbling and a stifled gasp. A quick look chilled her blood.

Jason dangled over the long drop to the rock-strewn bank of the Red by bleeding fingertips. A small trickle of pebbles and snaillike fossil shells rattled downward, leaving a trailing plume of brown dust cloud. She longed to help him, yet sensed that to try would be to doom them both. Slowly, his face contorted in pain, Jason powered himself upward by the bulging muscles of his arms and shoulders. His feet sought purchase . . . failed and searched again.

At last he got a toehold and relieved the strain on his tormented fingers and creaking muscles of his torso. He hugged the sheer wall, panting, a mighty, visible tremble coursing through him from shoulder to thigh. Long, tense seconds went by. Then he nodded.

"Take off your boots," Rebecca told him in a hushed voice. "It might hurt your feet some, but you can tell when you have a safe hold."

Three minutes more of climbing brought them both to the ledge. Jason's thick, woolen stockings had been worn to uselessness, and he removed them before replacing his boots. He mustered a smile and gave it to Rebecca.

"For a second there, I thought I wouldn't make it."

"So did I," she told him honestly. "From here on it should be easy. If I remember right, this path leads directly to the cave."

Opie Dillon studied his rear guard. He had the five remaining Comancheros, including their new leader, Jenkins, and four of his pals from the gang. Not a whole lot. He thought about the dynamite that Jenkins had along. There ought to be some way to make that useful. He took a swig from his canteen as his dim wits wrestled with the effort of forming a plan. A sudden increase in the volume of fire outside brought him to the front of the cave.

"They're makin' a rush," Jenkins told him.

"Pour it on, boys. We gotta hold 'em."

Opie added his fire to that of the others. The small figures grew larger as they fought among the rocks on a fan-shaped moraine that extended to the river's edge and provided the only route of attack. One man, a ranger Opie figured, from the shiny star on his vest, dropped to one knee, cursing and gripping at the bullet hole in his leg.

Opie took careful aim at the wounded ranger and

squeezed off a shot.

The ranger flipped backward and fell under a shower of his brains and blood. Slowly the attack faltered and the besiegers retreated to better protection.

"We have to keep pressing them," Lone Wolf insisted. "Taylor, take your men and Sir Devon and go up the same way. Tony here and I will take the opposite side of the fan. While they're all watching you, we ought to be able to get in position to fire directly on the men in the cave."

Lone Wolf and Lord Anthony Parrish started off first. The careful skills of a Crow warrior served Lone Wolf well. With a little instruction he insured that even the English lord would not leave telltale puffs of dust as they ascended the bulging moraine. To their left, shots began, telling of the rangers' new attack.

"Keep climbing," Lone Wolf commanded. "We're almost there."

Two minutes later he eased his head over the curve of the gigantic rubble pile and looked down on the slouched, dirty hats of the defenders. A smile creased his sun-bronzed cheeks. He beckoned Lord Anthony forward.

"There. Pick a target."

Their first shots created havoc in the cave. Two of the rear guard died without a sound, drilled through the tops of their heads. The thrashing bodies sent the others scurrying.

"Come back!" Lone Wolf heard a voice demanding. "They gonna get us iffin we don't fight."

"I got a better idea," another man shouted.

Lone Wolf and Anthony continued to fire into the cave. A moment later, the white warrior saw an object twirl through the air, trailing a thin stream of white smoke and a few sparks. It struck near the top of the moraine and a second later a sun-bright explosion bloomed.

With a mighty tremble, the earth began to move. Long Wolf reacted immediately.

"Rockslide. Run!" he shouted.

Stumbling and gasping, Lone Wolf and Anthony raced for the bottom of the shifting pile of rocks and debris. They didn't stop running until waist deep in the Red River. Seconds later Taylor and his rangers and Sir Devon joined them. A huge dust cloud obscured the entire cliff face and the rattle and rumble of cascading rock continued for long, tense minutes. At last it subsided.

"That sumbitch has got dynamite," Taylor observed as he spit a long, brown stream of tobacco juice into the disturbed water. "They got one of my boys. Covered him right up in that slide."

"We'll fix 'em. Don't worry about that," Lone Wolf promised with an assurance he had begun to doubt.

Nervous backward glances became more frequent for Opie Dillon. By the time the dynamite blast had interrupted operations on the part of their besiegers, even his dim brain had begun to perceive that Roger and Jake had abandoned them to secure their own escape. Rather than anger him, it only made him worry more. Something had to be done.

"That's the way, boys," he encouraged. "Jenkins, use some more of that dynamite. Keep their heads down. I think somethin's gone wrong. I wanna trace that route so we can get outta here. I'll be back shortly."

Opie took one of the extra torches constructed for

the escape route, set it to burning with a lucifer match, and entered the center chamber of the cave. Shadows leaped and writhed in the flickering light, and a cold dread began to seep out from his heart. The pictographs startled him and he tried to make sense of them. Stymied in this effort, he moved on.

He had to duck low to negotiate the passage into the third cavern. When he stood upright, Opie came face to face with the most frightening object he had ever encountered. The hackles rose on his neck at the sight of a gigantic figure, that of a bear, with a grinning Indian head on its short neck. Never slow when it came to shootin' irons, Opie reacted instantly.

His Colt cleared his belt and he blasted a slug into the petroglyph. The slug screamed off into the farther regions of the cave. The horrifying image remained in place, blocking his path.

"Oh! Oh, my God!" Opie gasped aloud. Frightened out of his sparse wits, with no clear idea of the escape route, he turned and hurried back toward the comfort and security of the other men.

She had been right. Rebecca felt a sense of relief well up in her breast as she and Jason closed the last few yards to a blind corner of the cave's mouth. Below she could see the small figures of the rangers. Among them she spotted Lone Wolf and waved to him. He made no reply but set about organizing another assault.

Men rushed up the slope, firing as they ran. Immediately, a large volume of return shots sounded. Amid the roar of gunfire, she heard a familiar voice.

"All right, you know what to do," Opie Dillon said in a ghostly echo.

At once the firing began to dwindle inside the cave.

216

Soon only two weapons barked in defiance of the assaulting force. Tight-lipped, Rebecca turned to Jason.

"This is it. We wait until Lone Wolf brings the rangers within a few feet of the cave, then we go in, too."

"I'm ready. And . . . once more, I want to say that I love you dearly."

"I . . . I love you, Jason. More than anyone in my life."

"We'll be all right, you'll see."

"Now. They're almost on top of it."

Rebecca and Jason ran around a protruding boulder and dashed a dozen short yards to the cave. Jason entered first.

A man knelt in the mouth, a bundle of dynamite sticks in his hands. He had just attached the cap and prepared to ignite the long, looping train of fuse. For a moment, both men froze in surprise. Then Jenkins set aside the large charge and went for his gun.

Unfamiliar with a handgun, Jason fumbled his draw. The front sight of the Smith and Wesson hung up, wedged against the holster, which gave Jenkins time to clear leather. Jason got the .44 free and began to swing it upward. Behind him, Rebecca entered the cavern as Jenkins eared back the hammer.

"Jason!" she shouted in warning.

Jenkins' shot slammed violently against their ears in the confines of the cave.

Jason lurched backward, his revolver falling from nerveless fingers. Color drained from his face and he turned his head aside, seeking the object of his words.

"R-Rebecca . . . I . . . do . . . lov . . ."

Jason Plumm, Lord Southington, fell dead, shot through the breast, a scant moment before Rebecca Caldwell put two bullets into Jenkins' face.

Hot lead from the smoking .44 in the white squaw's hand turned the Comanchero's head into mush. Blood and yellowish fluid sprayed from his ears as his eyes flew from their sockets, followed by a spew of brain matter, and he slammed back against the cave wall.

"You animal bastard!" she screamed as she pumped three more rounds into his jerking body. Then she sagged and went to her knees beside her dead love. Gently she cradled his head in her lap and began to sob.

"We still have to get the others," a familiar voice reminded her, ending her brief moment of sorrow. She looked appealingly up into Lone Wolf's grim face.

"He . . . he was so beautiful. Why, Lone Wolf? Why?"

"All is as the Great Spirit wills," he told her harshly. "Will you slash your arms and cut your braids?"

Her glazed eyes cleared and the fires of retribution blazed in the dark blue irises. "No. I'll find Jake Tulley and slowly roast his balls over a bed of coals. Let's not let them get away this time."

Only six men remained with Opie Dillon as they stood in the dark and listened to the reverberations of gunfire inside the cave. In the blackness his lip trembled, through none could see it. A moment before they had doused the torches to prevent the enemy from being led to them. In the instant they did, Opie had seen that only a blank face filled the space in front of them. A dead end.

"Turn around," he urged the others in a hoarse whisper. "We have to go back to that other branch-off."

Slowly the fleeing outlaws shuffled forward, arms extended to feel their way. A warmer breath of air

218

indicated to Opie that they had reached the chamber where the branch tunnels had been discovered. Sudden brightness flared from the direction of the main cave.

Opie turned to see two persons whom fear had so thoroughly branded into his memory. Rebecca Caldwell, a big revolver in one hand, and the man Lone Wolf. Weak with fright, Opie turned and staggered back as six-guns roared and drove spikes of pain into his ears.

Rebecca fired first. One of the fugitive bandits went down, clasping hands to his belly. She swung on another, a Comanchero, and shot him through the throat at the same moment Lone Wolf's Colt blasted beside her. A third man went down, hit in the heart, before a shot fired by one of the fleeing outlaws smashed the torch from Lone Wolf's hand and plunged the cavern into darkness.

Scuffling footsteps faded into the black interior of the cave as the survivors sought escape.

"I'll take those two," Lone Wolf told his companion. He headed away from her as she went after Opie Dillon.

Stygian velvet engulfed her and she paused a moment to listen. In the distance, Rebecca heard rough breathing. Two of them, she decided. Cautiously she went along the low, winding path of the passage. Her senses strained for any sign of danger, for some indication of the presence of the men she sought. She kept her left hand in contact with the wall as she inched her way along, consumed with impatience at the creeping pace.

She halted suddenly when she sensed that the breathing had stopped. No, not stopped exactly. With a tingle of dread, she realized that she had gone past the last point where she had heard the muffled gasps. The soft sound of rustling clothing brought her around in a flash.

A distant shot sounded as Lone Wolf finished off another of the fugitives. The unexpected noise caused her assailant to lose stride. The knife he carried scraped against the roof of the passage. In the same split second, Rebecca fired.

Muzzle flame lighted the low vault, and Rebecca saw a chunk of jaw fly away from the gunman's face. He shrieked with pain as she cocked the Smith and Wesson and triggered another lead messenger of death.

His wail of agony choked off in mid-screech, and Rebecca heard his body hit the floor. She turned about and moved on. A faint glow radiated from beyond a bend. She approached with caution and eased her head around the rough wall.

Rebecca saw that the passage she followed slanted downward, and a brighter circle of light beckoned to her. She broke open the .44 American and removed expended cartridges. These she pocketed and replaced them with new loads. With a full cylinder, she advanced along the nature-hewn corridor until she discovered that it opened into a medium-sized room.

Across the rubble-strewn floor, Opie Dillon cringed against the far wall. Those who had escaped with Tulley and Styles had left a torch, and its dwindling light flickered on his sallow, fear-tinged face. Six-gun at the ready, Rebecca advanced across the cave toward him.

"I-I-I . . . I di'n' mean nothin'," he whined when he recognized Rebecca. "W-why I didn't even vote to give you to them Injuns. Pu-puleze don' hurt me!"

"You walking bag of outhouse filth," Rebecca growled low in her throat. "Did you think I would forget? Do you believe that I could ever erase the memory or the feeling of your rough finger shoved up inside me? How you rubbed my butt up against tha

220

obscene bulge in your pants when you boosted me up behind Iron Calf? All those things you whispered in my ear that you wanted to do to me? Do you remember them?"

In a hard, grating voice, Rebecca enumerated every descriptive act of perversion and inversion that Opie Dillon had gloatingly suggested to her as an alternative to going with the Oglala on that day so long ago. All she had to do, he had crooned over and over, was open his fly and suck on that big, red ol' all-day sucker. Take it in every imaginable opening of her body. On and on she listed his spew of filth while his face sagged, and a green tinge circled his froth-flecked lips. At last she came to the end.

"Hurt you?" he heard her ask. "I can't think of anything vile enough to do to you. You have a gun there, Opie. Tucked right in the top of your trousers. I'll give you a fair chance to go for it."

Despite his emasculating fear, hope flamed up in Opie's chest. Slowly at first, then with desperate speed, his hand rose from his side toward the butt of the Colt jammed into his waistband.

Rebecca shot him through the back of his hand, smashing the fine bones before it slammed like a triphammer into his belly and ravaged his guts.

"Why!" he shrieked. "You said you'd give me a chance."

"Sometimes," she told the dying pervert in front of her through a sweet smile, "I lie a little."

Opie opened his mouth to scream, but Rebecca shot him through the diaphragm before it came out. Robbed of the ability to breathe, Opie Dillon worked his mouth like a beached fish and watched with fascinated horror while the beautiful young girl cocked the hammer a third time and rested the barrel on the bridge of his nose. His eyes crossed, staring at the muzzle.

"Good-bye, Opie."

Rebecca blew Opie's brains all over the wall of the cave.

Guided by the shots, the rest of the impromptu posse found Rebecca and they left the caves. Rebecca had a distant, glazed stare that seemed to focus on nothing. She didn't speak and let others lead her from place to place. Only when they reached the mouth of the cave did she pause. Her glance turned to the body of Jason Plumm and her mouth worked feebly a moment before she got the words out.

"G-good-bye, my dear, dear, Jason. If only you had not died in vain."

Wisely, Lone Wolf suggested that she be left alone with her grief. He made her a camp and withdrew with the other men. Once he saw Sir Devon and Lord Anthony on their way back to the English camp, sadly bearing the body of Jason Plumm, Lone Wolf hunted game, left part for Rebecca and took the rest to his own fire.

Three days later, he joined her and without comment on the tragedy she had endured, helped load gear on their pack mule.

"The trail is cold," he said simply.

"We'll find them," Rebecca replied with steely words. "Not even the halls of Hell can hide Jake Tulley from me. We'll find them again . . . and . . . then . . . they . . . shall pay."